The
Army Doctor's
Valentine's Baby

Helen Scott Taylor

Other Books in the Army Doctor's Series

Acknowledgments

As always, I would like to thank my critique partner Mona Risk for helping to improve the story and my son, Peter Taylor, for creating another lovely book cover. Thanks also to Leandra Hanes for stepping in to proofread for me and doing a fine job.

Chapter One

The insistent ring of the telephone dragged Captain Naomi Gray out of her dreams. She lay disoriented in the darkness for a moment before she remembered where she was. In the on-call room at the Army Institute of Thermal Medicine in the Scottish Highlands—also known as the back of beyond.

A glance at the clock told her it was four in the morning, Christmas Day. The institute was supposed to be closed for the holiday season. All the military personnel who staffed the place were on leave and had gone home to celebrate with their family and friends. All except for her and a few miserable security staff who had drawn the short straw.

She'd only slept in the on-call room as it was much warmer than her chilly army lodgings. Although she had stayed, she was still supposed to be on leave. Yet she couldn't ignore the call. With a little huff of resignation she reached for the phone. "Hello, Captain Gray."

"Sorry to disturb you, doc, but it's an emergency." She recognized the voice of one of the soldiers who'd been left on security detail.

"What is it, Smith?"

"A baby, ma'am."

"A baby?" Naomi sat up and rubbed her eyes.

1

"We've found one in a bag outside the gate. It was left right by the trash. Hate to think what would have happened if we hadn't heard it crying. It's gone quiet now, though."

His last comment galvanized Naomi into action. She jumped out of bed and dug through the heap of clothes on her chair, the phone still to her ear. "How old is it?"

"Newborn, I reckon, ma'am."

Naomi cursed softly under her breath. She'd heard of people abandoning babies outside hospitals, but this wasn't a normal hospital. The army institute was specialized and only treated patients with injuries sustained through cold.

"Okay. Bring the baby to reception. I'll meet you there in five."

She dropped the phone, dragged on her thick fleece jacket and jog pants over her pajamas, then pulled on a white coat over the top. She didn't have time to dress properly. A tiny baby left out in sub-zero temperatures was likely to be suffering from hypothermia.

Jamming her bare feet into sneakers, Naomi burst out of the door, running, the motion lights popping on along the hall as she passed. Luckily the institute was on a small scale and the reception area was not far.

Smith waited for her where she'd told him. He'd put a supermarket carrier bag on the reception desk and was leaning over it. "She was wriggling when we first found her, but she's gone very still now, doc. Hope she's all right."

Inside the carrier bag lay a crumpled bundle, a tiny, naked newborn baby wrapped in a cream blanket surrounded by layers of newspaper. At least whoever abandoned the baby had tried to insulate her against the cold. But the poor little soul was so thin she had no subcutaneous fat to provide thermal insulation.

Naomi grabbed her stethoscope from her pocket and put in the ear pieces, then lifted aside the baby's cover and pressed the diaphragm over the newborn's heart to check the apical pulse. Her fingers brushed the child's cold skin and she swallowed back her worry. Thank God there was a heartbeat. She prayed she would be able to warm the baby in time to save her life. She had no experience with neonatal medicine and would have to depend on common sense.

"Call Colonel Mackenzie and tell him what's happened. Tell him we'll need some newborn-size diapers, baby clothes, some formula, and a bottle." And good luck to her boss on getting hold of those things in the early hours of Christmas morning.

In a pediatric unit the baby would probably be put in an incubator under a radiant lamp to warm up. They didn't have such a thing here. She grabbed the handles of the bag and jogged back up the hall towards the on-call room.

One thing she did know was that the child must not be warmed too quickly, or the peripheral blood vessels would expand and it could lead to a fall in blood pressure in the baby's vital organs.

She lifted the tiny bundle of life from the bag and her heart contracted with pain on the child's behalf. Who could abandon such a sweet, vulnerable little girl? Working quickly, Naomi tucked the baby under the covers of her bed. She pulled a thermometer from the pocket of her white coat.

Naomi dragged off the clothes she'd worn over her pajamas and climbed into bed beside the tiny girl. She lifted her pajama top and gasped at the chill as she laid the cold, naked child on her belly. In the awkward confines of the bed, she slipped the thermometer beneath the newborn's arm to take her axillary temperature.

"It's all right, sweetheart. You're safe now. I'll look after you." Naomi had no idea if the child could hear her, but if she could the sound of a voice might be

3

comforting.

The little body twitched, giving Naomi hope. She held the baby close, counting off the seconds until it was time to read the thermometer.

She slipped it out and held it up to the light. The reading was only just below normal at 36.1 degrees centigrade. Setting the thermometer aside, she cuddled the naked baby, skin to skin, using her body heat to warm the child as quickly as she dared. Gradually the baby's pale color pinked and a mewling cry came from the tiny girl's lips.

Snuggled in bed with the baby against her chest in the warm cocoon beneath the covers, Naomi softly sang nursery rhymes she remembered from school. She had never wanted children, never even considered it a possibility. Yet as she cuddled the little girl to her chest, felt the newborn's small movements, and the soft brush of her breath against her skin, a twinge of longing stole through her.

She'd always thought babies and family were not for her. Her mother had not exactly set her a good example. But maybe one day she might think about having a baby. One day, a long time in the future, when she'd fulfilled her dream of traveling the world with the army.

A knock on the door made her jump.

"Naomi, are you in there?" Her commanding officer's voice rang out.

"Come in, sir."

Col. Duncan Mackenzie, the only thing that made this posting in dreary Scotland bearable, poked his head around the door. His dark hair was a little disheveled and a shadow of stubble darkened his jaw, making him look very masculine and sexy. His usual easy smile was absent, lines of worry marring his forehead.

"Where's the baby?"

"In bed. I'm warming her with my body heat, sir."

His eyebrows rose as he stepped inside. "Well done. That was sensible."

"Axillary temperature is only slightly below normal, sir. She's moving now and making a noise." As if to confirm Naomi's comment, the baby let out a wail.

"Can I see her?"

Naomi hesitated, suddenly self conscious at the prospect of revealing her naked belly. She would never jeopardize her career by acting on it, but she had a bit of a crush on her commanding officer.

She swallowed and lifted aside the bed covers, revealing the tiny baby girl curled up against her bare skin.

"Oh, my." Duncan crouched and touched his fingertips to the baby's back. His expression softened, his warm, dark eyes crinkling at the corners, his lips lifting into a smile. "She's a sweetheart."

Naomi's heart pounded with Duncan so close to her, gazing at her while she lay in bed.

Duncan took the baby's temperature again, then borrowed Naomi's stethoscope to check her heartbeat. He grasped a tiny foot in his hand. "Color is good and the child's extremities have warmed up too. You did well, Captain Gray. She's not cold now."

Duncan rested a hand on Naomi's shoulder, something he occasionally did as a gesture of support and praise. His touch had the strangest effect on her, as if electricity flowed from him and tingled along her nerves.

His glance moved from the baby to her face. He held her gaze for a moment, then he seemed to remember where they were. Clearing his throat, he stood and stepped back.

He was what people meant when they talked about a tower of strength. He was the sort of man who would never let down his child like her father had.

***

Naomi's pajama top was hitched up to just beneath her bust, her blonde hair spread across the pillow in a wild arc of gold. Duncan's gaze caught her's, the mesmerizing green of her eyes trapping him for a moment.

He pulled his gaze away from the strangely enticing sight of Naomi with the tiny newborn curled on her belly. He was treading on thin ice here. Those eyes filled his dreams most nights, tempting him. He already found it hard to concentrate in the OR during surgery when all he could see between her mask and cap were those green eyes framed by thick eyelashes.

He always maintained professional distance with his female staff. It had never been a problem before. But Naomi threatened to make him break all his rules.

To give himself time to recover his wits, he glanced away to set down the bag of baby items he'd collected from his sister's house on the way here.

"You managed to get some baby things?" Naomi asked. Her low, sexy purr of a voice didn't help matters either. She could make the blandest comment sound enticing. What was it about her that made every man in the institute worship the ground she walked on? It was more than her looks and voice. She had a certain charisma that drew men to her like wasps to marmalade.

"Enough," he whispered under his breath, annoyed with himself for this weakness. He was not a teenager ruled by his hormones but a man in his thirties who should know better. Naomi was in her mid-twenties, far too young for him anyway.

He dug in the bag and pulled out a tiny diaper and some cream. "Shall we put this on before she has an accident in your bed?"

Naomi laughed. "Good idea." She sat and lifted the baby in her arms, easing down her top to cover up, but not before he glimpsed an expanse of smooth, creamy skin that kicked up his pulse rate.

He focused on the baby. She opened her tiny bow of a mouth and cried. "That's a good sign," he said.

"Yes. It's a relief." Naomi glanced up, pleasure twinkling in her eyes. "She was so pale and still when security brought her in."

"I checked with Smith when he called. He didn't see the bag the child was in when he started his shift, so she can't have been out there for long. By the look of the tiny little thing that's lucky. If they hadn't found her quickly, she wouldn't have survived in the freezing temperatures."

"Shh, precious. Shh," Naomi said. Let's get you dressed up all warm and snuggly, and you can have something to eat."

She laid the baby on the bed. He passed the diaper across and watched her put it on. Then she dressed the little girl in a vest and pink sleep suit decorated with elephants. "Cute," she said.

Duncan glanced around the on-call room, noticing for the first time that Naomi had made herself at home here. Little frilly items of clothing and toiletries lay around, along with her laptop. "Are you living in this room?"

She glanced down sheepishly. "I hope you don't mind, sir. I've been sleeping here. It's warmer than my place."

Concern flashed through Duncan. "If the heating in your apartment's broken, we need to get someone to fix it." He'd been uncomfortable leaving Naomi here alone over Christmas. She was supposed to be on leave like the rest of his staff, but didn't seem to have anywhere to go.

"Don't worry until after Christmas." Naomi laughed, wryly. "I must be the only doctor in history who enjoys sleeping in the on-call room."

Naomi picked the baby up and swayed back and forth, murmuring to her as she fussed, obviously hungry.

"I'll ask maintenance to check your heating as soon as they're back after the holiday." Duncan still wasn't happy about her camping out in the on-call room for her leave. He had a duty of care to those under his command. Leaving her here alone over Christmas didn't sit right with him.

Frowning in thought, he grabbed the can of formula, and the bottle and headed along the corridor to the kitchen. Naomi followed him, swaying as she walked to soothe the baby. Duncan tried not to watch as she sashayed along, hips swinging. He normally only saw her in uniform. It was distracting when she was clad in baby blue pajamas covered in tiny sheep.

As he prepared the formula she watched closely. She was a fast learner. He'd been impressed that although she was an anesthetist, she had quickly picked up the testing protocols and treatment regime for cold injury. She was a bright young woman and would soon rise through the ranks given the chance.

"We'll have to call social services to fetch her, won't we?" she said, a note of resignation in her voice. She obviously didn't like that idea.

"Or we take her to the nearest general hospital, but that's quite a drive and there's more snow forecast. I'll call my friend Lyall in a minute. He's the local policeman. I'll see what he says, but I think the best course of action is for me to take her home once we've fed her. My brother Blair can take a look at her. He's an army pediatrician. She can stay with us for a few days. After Christmas, we'll pass her to social services to find her a foster home."

"Oh." Naomi's expression dropped. She pressed her lips together, then forced a smile. "Good idea, sir."

Duncan tested the temperature of the milk on his

wrist. "Okay, this is ready. Why don't you give it to her?" They traipsed back to the on-call room. Naomi sat in the easy chair, the baby in one arm, and angled the bottle into the newborn's mouth. After a couple of attempts the child latched onto the nipple and sucked.

"Good," Duncan said softly, pleased to see the child feeding.

While Naomi was busy, he pulled out his mobile phone and dialed Lyall's number to officially report finding the baby. The police would start searching for the mother, but nothing much would happen until after Christmas.

Lyall agreed that Duncan should bring the baby home. Naomi seemed to have taken to the little one and obviously wanted to look after her.

"What are your plans for today?" he asked.

Naomi gave a shrug.

"Come to Kindrogan with the baby if you like. You'll be able to help me with her." He purposely gave her a reason to come. It wasn't quite an order, but he injected a note of command in his voice.

She hesitated only a moment. "Yes, sir, of course. If I can be of help."

She did help him, in a way she would never suspect. When he was with Naomi, the emptiness inside him went away for a while.

Naomi Gray was beautiful, bright and eager to do well, always the first to volunteer to help. But occasionally Duncan caught a look of such sadness on her face it cut right to his core. She was good at putting on a front, but Naomi was not happy. More than anything, Duncan wanted to banish that sadness from her eyes.

Chapter Two

While Naomi tossed some clothes in a bag, Duncan found a plastic box in which they could carry the baby. He placed it on the bed and Naomi padded it with a folded towel, then placed the little one inside, tightly wrapped in a blanket.

"Ready?" Duncan asked, dropping the spare baby things back in the bag.

Naomi glanced around the cozy room that she'd adopted as her own, almost sad to leave. Although when everyone came back after Christmas, and it became the on-call room again, she wouldn't be able to stay here. She'd have to return to her dingy, cold army apartment.

All her friends who'd passed out with her at the end of their officer's training at The Royal Military Academy Sandhurst had been posted to interesting places like Germany, Gibraltar, Cyprus, and Canada, while she'd been stuck with wretched Scotland. She hadn't even made it off British soil.

Naomi sucked in a breath and blew it out. With a bit of luck she wouldn't be here for much longer. She'd already put in for a transfer.

She nodded. "I'm ready."

Duncan carried the baby in the plastic box. Naomi followed with the bags. They turned off the lights and locked up, making sure the place was secure.

The chill hit Naomi and she shivered as she stepped

outside. Shoveled snow lay in heaps around the perimeter fence. In the faint light from the first streaks of dawn, a sheen of frost sparkled across the car park.

Duncan opened the back door of his vehicle, a Land Rover with Kindrogan Estate emblazoned across the side. He stowed the baby's box on the back seat, secured it with a seat belt, and tugged the strap to make sure it was safe. "Not ideal," he said, "but the best we can do without a baby car seat."

He opened the passenger door for her, then climbed in and started the engine. Private Smith saluted as they drove out of the gate. Duncan cracked open his side window. "Merry Christmas, Smith."

"Merry Christmas to you too, sir."

They drove in silence, the headlights cutting through the shadows, picking out the huge metal trash bins where the baby had been found. Within a few minutes they reached the main street of Kinder Vale. Christmas decorations sparkled around doors and in windows. On the green outside the village hall a tall Christmas tree glowed with tiny lights, casting multicolored streaks of light across the snowy ground.

"The weather forecast says we're due more snow, sir," Naomi said, when the silence grew awkward. Although she wanted to look after the baby, she wasn't sure how she felt about spending Christmas day at Duncan's home. Christmas had always been an uncomfortable time, spent with people who didn't want her there. She had hoped to avoid that this year.

She felt like a cuckoo in the nest when she visited her mum or dad's new families. She was much older than her step brothers and sisters, and her parents' new partners made no secret of the fact they didn't want her around.

"We're used to snow here." Duncan glanced her way, light gleaming off his eyes for a moment. "You're from London, aren't you?"

"Originally." Naomi hoped he wouldn't ask any more questions about home. She always hated having to lie and pretend things had been okay. She'd rather not talk about her past at all.

Duncan obviously got the message as he fell silent again. They turned down a rough lane between pine woodland and bumped along the road, then crested a hill. Below lay Loch Kinder. In the dawn light, mist hung over the surface of the water like something out of a fairy tale. Kindrogan Castle with its towers and crenellated battlements stood at the far end, flanked by the dark peaks of the mountains, silhouetted against the lightening sky.

Naomi held her breath, uncertainty washing through her. She cast Duncan a quick sideways glance, just able to make out his face. She was used to treating Duncan with respect, he was a colonel, her commanding officer, but the reality of his family life hadn't really occurred to her. Not only was his father a brigadier, he was the local laird. They were aristocracy. She would have to be on best behavior.

"Can the baby sleep with me?" That would give her an excuse to retreat to her room if she felt uncomfortable.

"I don't see why not. She'll need to be with one of us so we can keep an eye on her."

Duncan drove the vehicle along the narrow road around the loch, then past the castle and pulled up in the courtyard at the back. "Here we are. Home."

He climbed out and came around to open her door, and give her a hand down. Naomi grabbed the two bags and waited while Duncan fetched the baby from the back seat. She followed him in through the back door.

Blinking Christmas lights strung around the high ceiling illuminated an old fashioned kitchen. A large wooden table stood in the centre with a holly-trimmed candle in the center, a dresser and wooden cabinets around the walls.

Two Westies leaped up from their beds in the corner and jumped up at Duncan, tails wagging, as he placed the baby's box on the table. "Good boys." He rubbed behind their ears and patted them. "Meet Bruce and Torrie."

"Hello, you two fluff balls." Naomi crouched to stroke them. She had longed for a dog when she was young, but there'd been no chance of that.

"My brother Blair's here, but he'll have a lie-in today. I suggest we catch a couple more hours of sleep while the baby's settled. You can stay in my sister's old room."

Naomi followed Duncan along a corridor into an entrance hall, the high ceiling disappearing into shadow. The stairs creaked as they climbed past a row of old portraits. At the top, Duncan led her to the left, opened a bedroom door and switched on the light.

The large room had flowery drapes and light wood furniture carved with a pretty pattern of Celtic knots. Naomi put her bag on the end of the bed while Duncan placed the baby in her box on a chest of drawers.

He felt the top of the radiator. "Baby should be warm enough in here. The bed's made up. You get another couple of hours sleep. When the child wakes my brother can examine her to make sure she's all right. Where the cord was cut might need attention. Apart from that she seems fine to me, but it won't hurt to have a pediatrician check her over."

"Thanks. The room's lovely."

Duncan pointed across the corridor. "Bathroom's opposite."

He bent over the baby and smiled. "Fast asleep, but not for long, I suspect. She's bound to be hungry again soon." He straightened.

"See you later." With a smile, he headed for the door, stepped out, and closed it softly behind him.

Naomi stood for a moment in the silent room, a sense of unreality floating through her. A few short hours ago she'd been minding her own business, fast asleep in the on-call room. Now here she was at Kindrogan Castle to spend Christmas day with her commanding officer and his family. And she was caring for a baby. She wandered across and stared down at the tiny squashed face of the newborn girl, sleeping as peacefully as if she didn't have a care in the world.

The poor little soul had lots of challenges ahead if she went into the care system. Naomi knew firsthand how stressful and upsetting it was. She wished she could spare this little angel that experience and find her a loving home.

Despite Duncan's suggestion to Naomi that they should catch a few more hours sleep, he did not go back to bed. A strange restlessness assailed him. He stopped at the top of the stairs and tapped his fingers on the stair rail, wondering if Blair was awake. But the house was silent, the only sound the steady tick of the grandfather clock in the front hall.

Normally when he felt like this, he buried himself in paperwork in his office. There was always plenty to do. His brother, Hew, managed the practical running of Kindrogan Estate, but there were not enough hours in the day for him to do everything.

Duncan rose at six each morning to deal with the estate admin before he left for the army institute. He spent most evenings in the office as well. Having plenty of time to himself was one good thing about not having a wife and children—the only good thing as far as he was concerned.

He ran down the creaky stairs of this place he loved like an old friend. A place where he assumed he would one day bring a bride. Where he thought his children would grow up, enjoying the fun of running free in the countryside, shooting, fishing, hiking, skiing, doing all the things he and his siblings had loved. But that special woman who would make his life complete had not shown up.

Last summer his sister Megan had been married and now had a baby. He was delighted to see her so happy, but her domestic bliss only served to highlight how empty his life was. He thought he'd come to terms with being alone. Now he realized he hadn't.

He walked into the kitchen, pulled on his jacket and jammed his feet in rubber boots, then whistled to the dogs, and headed out the back door. Dawn colored the sky pink with pale gold streaks, like the watercolor pictures Hew painted.

With Torrie and Bruce scampering everywhere, sniffing the early morning smells, Duncan paced around the side of the castle and headed for the loch. The yellow disc of the winter sun fought its way through the usual blanket of cloud that draped the surrounding mountains, and painted the rippling water with light.

Duncan's breath misted before him as he walked along the bank to a small rocky cove no more than twelve feet long that offered a private place on the edge of the water. He leaned back against the cold granite, staring into the distance, over the cloak of mist draping the valleys, and across the spiky tops of Caledonian pine trees.

This had been a favorite place of his since childhood. He and Blair had built camp fires to cook sausages on the small pebble beach.

In the warmer weather they'd camped on the grass nearby and rowed out on the loch where old Angus, his father's gillie, had taught them how to fish. Eventually Hew had been old enough to join them. Duncan had been the one to teach him to fish and hunt. He'd looked forward to sharing all this with his own children.

15

Bruce jumped up at Duncan, pasting dirty, wet pawmarks on his jeans. He smiled, used to such things and not caring. You couldn't live at Kindrogan and worry about a little dirt. He pulled a ball from his pocket and tossed it across the rough grass. Both dogs took off, their short legs pumping as they raced each other for the prize. As usual Bruce got there first and snatched up the ball, charging off with Torrie on his heels, barking.

Duncan sucked in a long breath of cool air flavored with the essence of Scotland, something wild and natural, beautiful and indefinable. Something he loved above all else.

This life at Kindrogan was a gift that few were lucky enough to experience. He longed to share this with a woman he loved.

The dogs rushed through some reeds and sent a pair of Goldeneye squawking into the air. The ducks flew farther out, skimming the water, landing on the gleaming surface, fluffing up their feathers and shaking their heads in a show of displeasure.

What did Naomi think of Kindrogan? Would she be happy to live here?

There was something about her that resonated with him, something he hadn't felt since he was a student. Back then he'd fallen in love with a young woman whose mother worked at Kindrogan. His father had said it was an abuse of position to date the daughter of a member of staff.

Duncan had done the right thing and tried to forget her, but he'd never felt drawn to another woman that strongly until now, until Naomi Gray arrived at the army institute.

Once again he was bound by the same code of behavior. He'd suppressed his feelings for Naomi for nearly a year. Now she had applied for another posting. Duncan had approved the request, even though he hadn't wanted to. In four to six weeks she'd be gone.

Time was running out to tell her how he felt. He had to make his move now, or lose her forever.

Chapter Three

Naomi woke to the mewling cry of a tiny baby. She sat up, a smile on her face as she glanced at the plastic box, serving as the child's temporary crib. A little burst of pleasure and anticipation shot through her as she slid out of bed and crossed the room.

The tiny girl stared up at Naomi through cornflower blue eyes, her wispy blonde hair soft as thistle down beneath Naomi's fingertips. "You are an adorable little poppet, aren't you?"

The baby had Naomi's coloring. She might almost be Naomi's own child. The thought made her catch her breath with a strange mix of emotions. To be solely responsible for a tiny newborn was a frightening prospect. For the first time, she had a glimmer of how overwhelmed her mother must have felt to have that responsibility when she was only sixteen.

A little of Naomi's resentment towards her mother faded. But she was a long way from forgiving her parents for how they had treated her.

"Shall we go and find you a bottle of milk, sweetie?" She gathered the tiny girl in her arms, cradling her head in a palm. She was so small and fragile, so in need of loving care that it squeezed Naomi's heart.

She padded barefoot out of her room and down the stairs, the bag containing the bottle and formula hooked over her arm. It was a bit chilly dressed only in her pajamas but she wouldn't be long. All she had to do was prepare the bottle. Then she could head back to her nice warm bedroom and snuggle in bed with the baby while she fed her.

The house lay still and silent, but the smell of roasting turkey reached her as she descended the stairs, so someone was up.

On silent feet she traversed the entrance hall, noticing the coat of arms over the front door, and ancient weapons hung high on the wood-paneled walls. What an unusual place to live, but not an uncomfortable one. She headed to the kitchen where she had entered a few hours earlier. Halting at the kitchen doorway, she peered in to check if anyone was there.

Duncan stood at the counter, a mug in his hand, staring out the window towards the courtyard, obviously lost in thought. Faded jeans clung to his lean hips, a checked flannel shirt, and padded vest covering his torso. Today was the first time she'd seen him in anything apart from army uniform. He looked good.

He was a big man, tall and broad. She was five foot eight and he had at least eight inches on her. Yet he was a kind and gentle man, a man dedicated to helping his patients. When she left the army institute, she would miss him.

The baby made a snuffling sound and Duncan swung around. His gaze roamed over her, dark and brooding. Heat pulsed between them, as if the very air crackled. Naomi blinked in surprise. In all the months she'd known him, he'd never looked at her like *this* before.

"Good...good morning, sir," she stuttered.

"Call me Duncan. We're off duty now, Naomi."

"Okay. Good morning, Duncan."

"That's better. I like the PJ's by the way. You make a

19

bonnie picture first thing in the morning." He came closer. With a smile he took the bag off her arm to pull out the bottle and formula. "I imagine the little lass is hungry again." He clicked on the electric kettle and pulled a glass jug from a cupboard.

Tingling all over, acutely aware of Duncan as a man rather than just her boss, Naomi stared at him, uncertain what to make of this subtle shift in the atmosphere between them.

"The turkey smells good," she said, trying to distract her thoughts.

"I switched the oven on awhile ago. The housekeeper left a schedule of what pans to turn on when. She left everything prepared."

"Helpful."

"Aye, very. I'm not much of a cook. Why don't you take the bairn back to your room where it's warm? I'll bring up the bottle when it's ready."

Before she could leave, footsteps sounded behind her. She turned to find a man who resembled Duncan but leaner, with darker hair, and blue eyes.

His eyebrows rose. "Good morning." His gaze passed over her then moved to Duncan. "Is there something you haven't told me, or is this beautiful woman a figment of my imagination?"

"Naomi, meet my brother Blair."

"The charming, good-looking brother," Blair added with a roguish grin.

"Naomi Gray. I work with Duncan at the army institute."

Blair angled his head to see the baby's face. "Yours, Ms. Gray?"

"It's Captain Gray and no, she was abandoned outside the institute in the early hours of the morning."

Immediately the expression on Blair's face transformed from charming flirt to concerned doctor. "How long was she outside?"

"Not long," Duncan said. "Naomi warmed her up. We think she's fine, but if you can check her over after she's fed, that might be a good idea." Duncan finished preparing the bottle, and picked it up along with a mug.

"Of course. Just give me a shout when you're ready," Blair said.

"Let's go up." Duncan raised the mug at Naomi. "I've made you a cup of tea."

Her gaze collided with Blair's curious look as they walked past. It hadn't occurred to her that Duncan's family would think they were a couple. Duncan's warm hand settled on her back and steadied her as she mounted the stairs with the baby in her arms. For a moment, she let herself imagine she *was* Duncan's girlfriend, and she belonged in this grand castle.

A strange sense of confusion swept through her. She had been certain that her goal in life was to see the world. That's mainly why she'd joined the army. A frisson of doubt whispered across her mind as she cuddled the baby with Duncan's reassuring touch on her back.

For the first time since she started studying medicine, the future didn't seem quite so clear.

"That was a lovely meal. Thank you." Naomi had thought she might be uncomfortable sharing Christmas dinner with a close-knit family like the Mackenzie's, but they were all friendly and made an effort to include her in their conversation. It helped that Sir Robert Mackenzie, who sounded a little intimidating, was away.

"Hear, hear," Duncan's sister, Megan, said from the other side of the huge oak table in the dining room. Her voice echoed into the beams of the lofty ceiling where pine garlands trimmed with red and gold baubles hung. "You did an excellent job, Duncan. Mrs. Stewart will make a cook of you yet."

"Not if I can help it," Duncan retorted and everybody laughed. "Anyway, all I did was twist a few knobs on the cooker."

"Well you twisted them well, laddie," Megan added.

Naomi glanced behind her to check the abandoned baby, now more comfortably housed in a white, lace-trimmed bassinette that Duncan's brother Hew had brought. Apparently it had belonged to his son, Fergus, who was now three. The little boy sat between his father and his Aunt Megan on the other side of the table, a miniature version of the Mackenzie brothers.

Megan's five week old baby girl, Heather, let out a wail and started crying. "Uh, oh. We're hungry again, aren't we, darling."

Megan's husband, Maj. Daniel Fabian, stood and picked up the little girl from her baby seat on the table behind him. He was a skilled surgeon who worked at the institute with Naomi. It was strange seeing him out of uniform, rocking his daughter in his arms, adoration on his face.

"Well, I don't think I could eat another thing." Blair leaned back in his chair and patted his belly. "I might manage a wee dram though, if there's one forthcoming." He glanced at Duncan hopefully.

"I vote we women go to the drawing room to feed the babies in peace and you men clear up," Megan announced. "What do you think, Naomi?"

They all glanced her way and she blushed. "Well, I don't mind helping to clear up."

Duncan smiled and rested a hand on her arm. "No. You're our guest. You go with Meg and we'll be through in a while. There's a full bottle of formula ready in the fridge. You just need to heat it in the bottle warmer that Hew brought over."

"The abandoned baby is very good. When did you last feed her?" Megan said.

"Four hours ago." They'd started referring to the

rescued baby this way to differentiate her from Megan's little girl. But Naomi hated calling her abandoned, even though it was true. "We need a name for the baby," she said.

"Kinder," Blair suggested. "She was found in the Kinder Valley."

Naomi angled her head, thinking about this suggestion. It was good but somehow the name didn't suit the little girl. Although how she knew it didn't suit when the baby was only a few hours old she had no idea.

"Holly." Hew picked up a sprig of holly that had decorated the top of the Christmas pudding and twirled it between his fingers.

"Yes," Naomi and Duncan said in unison. Silence fell across the room as everyone looked at them. Naomi averted her gaze from the speculative glances. Duncan's family definitely thought there was something going on between them.

Megan broke the silence. "I like that too. She was born on Christmas day, after all."

"Holly it is," Duncan replied, his gaze meeting Naomi's. A strange rush of sensation swept though her. For a moment she forgot the curiosity of his family. At work, she'd kept a lid on her crush for Duncan, but now they were off duty the boundaries had faded. What had seemed impossible no longer did.

Hew stood and started loading dishes from the table onto a wheeled trolley. Blair and Megan's husband traded stories of the places they had been skiing and snowboarding, a definite tone of one-upmanship to their banter. Duncan silently gathered up the plates.

"Will you watch Holly for a moment? I'll fetch her bottle," Naomi said.

Duncan nodded.

Naomi hurried across the entrance hall and headed along the corridor towards the kitchen. She took a moment alone there as she waited for the bottle to heat. The wonderful cooking smells lingered, but a mountain of dirty pots and pans filled the sink. The men were going to be here for a while. As the bottle warmer dinged, the squeaky wheels of the trolley sounded in the hall.

Naomi grabbed the bottle. With a quick smile she crossed with the men as they headed towards the kitchen.

"I've put Holly in the drawing room," Duncan said.

"Thanks. Good luck with the washing up."

The drawing room was like an historic film set come to life, with ancient hunting trophies, shields, and swords on the walls, and antique furniture that should probably be in a museum. A huge Christmas tree sparkling with glass baubles and tinsel garlands stood in the corner.

Megan sat on a chair in front of the roaring log fire, her baby at her breast. She gazed down at her daughter, an expression of such contentment on her face that Naomi envied her.

Megan glanced up and smiled. "Feeding Heather is a good excuse for a few moments peace. I love my husband dearly, but he and Blair talk nonstop. Poor Duncan and Hew can't get a word in edgeways, nor can I for that matter."

Naomi laughed as she picked Holly up and settled in the corner of a large, comfy sofa near Megan. "I noticed."

She peeled the blanket back from the baby's tiny body so she wouldn't get too hot in front of the fire, then settled her in the crook of her arm, and put the nipple in her mouth. Blair had checked her over earlier and given her a clean bill of health.

"So what's the deal with you and Duncan?" Megan asked.

"Nothing. I'm only here to look after Holly."

Megan chortled. "So all the longing gazes Duncan's been giving you were my imagination."

Naomi's eyes widened as she took that in. "Really?"

"Oh, yes. I know my brother. He's smitten."

Pleasure rushed through Naomi. She looked down, trying to suppress the grin stretching her lips.

"Don't hurt him, will you? It's not often he falls for someone. In fact I can't remember the last time."

"No, of course I won't." She hadn't knowingly done anything to lead him on. Although the thought that Duncan was interested in her set her nerves sparking like fireworks. How should she let him know that she returned his feelings? She was more used to rebuffing men than leading them on.

"It would be wonderful if you married Duncan. I've always wanted a sister."

Whoa. Naomi physically recoiled in her seat at the M word. Having a relationship was one thing, marriage was another altogether. She wasn't ready to tie herself down. She had a world to explore first.

"Well, I'm going up the wooden hill. I'll leave you to take care of sleeping beauty." Blair nodded towards Naomi, curled in the corner of the sofa, dead to the world.

"Goodnight," Duncan said.

Blair grabbed his empty whiskey glass and headed off, leaving Duncan in the drawing room. Duncan rested his head back on the chair and watched Naomi, a pleasant haze of contentment settling over him.

Megan and Daniel had departed much earlier to take their baby home to bed. Hew and Fergus had left at about the same time. Duncan, Blair, and Naomi then spent the evening chatting in front of the fire, and sipping fine double malt.

Now the fire had burned down to glowing embers that cast a warm light across the room, turning Naomi's golden hair to a fiery halo. She was so beautiful, delicate and pretty, but strong and determined as well. The perfect combination to make a good wife and mistress of Kindrogan.

Although he was getting ahead of himself. He hadn't even kissed her yet. But he intended to put that right soon.

As Naomi slept on, probably lulled by the whiskey she'd tried, Holly woke and let out a mewling cry. Duncan rose and went to the bassinette, set on a table away from the direct heat of the fire. "Hey there, you cute wee lassie. Is it food you're wanting?"

He stroked the tips of his fingers gently over her belly and chest, touching the palms of her tiny hands, smiling with pleasure when her fingers closed around his digit.

"You're a clever girl, aren't you, Holly." He liked that name. It suited her well. The image of a toddler with blonde hair and blue eyes, running around outside flitted through his mind. He shook his head at the direction of his thoughts. She wasn't his. The police would eventually track down her mother and try to reunite her with Holly.

He strode to the kitchen, warmed a bottle, and returned to the drawing room, half expecting Naomi to have been woken by Holly's cries, but she was still asleep.

He set the bottle down, lifted the baby into his arms, and settled in an armchair to feed her. He'd bottle-fed Fergus when he was tiny, and he had no trouble remembering how to do the same for Holly.

Once she'd finished and been burped, he cradled her in one arm, and picked up the bassinette with the other before taking the baby up to Naomi's bedroom. He changed Holly's diaper and settled her in her bed, snuggling her beneath the blankets and smoothing the soft blonde wisps of hair on her head. Then he trod quietly back downstairs.

Naomi lay where he'd left her, still fast asleep. Perhaps she'd drunk more whiskey than he thought? Perching on the sofa at her side, he ran a finger over the back of one of her slender hands.

"Naomi." Duncan pitched his voice softly, not wanting to wake her with a start. She didn't rouse. "Hey, sleeping beauty, time for bed." He skimmed a finger across her cheek, relishing the softness of her skin beneath his touch. No reaction.

He didn't intend to leave her in the drawing room all night. She'd wake with a stiff neck from her awkward position. His only option was to carry her upstairs.

Duncan slid one arm beneath her knees and the other around her back, lifting her floppy body against his chest, her head on his shoulder. He was halfway to the door when she finally blinked and opened her eyes.

"Duncan, oh, what's happening?"

He kept going, a grin on his lips. "I'm carrying you up to bed, milady."

"Gosh, no, I'm too heavy. Put me down."

Now he had hold of her, there was no way he would put her down before he reached her room. He was enjoying the feel of her in his arms too much. "Darling, I was caber tossing champion at the Scottish Highland Games two years running. Believe me, you are nowhere near as heavy as a tree trunk."

She relaxed into his arms, her eyelids drooping again. She wasn't really fully awake. He eyed the sprig of mistletoe Angus had tacked on the thick wooden lintel above the front door.

Duncan changed direction and headed that way. "This isn't the stairs," Naomi mumbled.

"No," Duncan said, his voice gruff at the thought of kissing her. "I've a little diversion in mind." He halted beneath the tiny green leaves and their clump of white berries, then watched her eyes widen as she noticed.

"I'd like a Christmas kiss, lass." If she said no he would honor her wishes and just take her upstairs. She blinked at him, a soft, languid expression on her face.

Lowering his head, he savored the moment, inhaling her sweet, floral fragrance before he pressed his lips to hers. Heat flared between them, running along his veins like molten lava, threatening to scorch his socks. He lifted his head, staring down at her, a wee bit shaken. Neither of them spoke, as if there were no words for what had just happened between them.

He continued up the stairs, his legs not quite as steady after that kiss. When he reached her bedroom door he set her on her feet, and smoothed the hair back off her face. He wanted to go inside so much he dared not.

"Holly's fed, changed and in bed," he whispered, cupping her cheek in his hand. He should say goodnight, walk away, let Naomi think about the first kiss before he tried for another. But good sense deserted him. He touched his lips to hers again. Her arms came around his neck, and he sank into the kiss. Lord help him, he was going to miss her when she left.

Chapter Four

Naomi slept restlessly, dreaming about the feel of Duncan's arms around her, the taste of his lips on hers. She stirred, thrilled and excited one moment, confused the next. For so long she'd been focused on her career, on her ticket to independence. Relationships had taken a back seat.

Since she was posted to the army institute nearly a year ago, she'd done her best to ignore her feelings for Duncan. She wasn't used to this overwhelming attraction to a man, this draw that made her wish she could be snuggled in bed beside him rather than alone.

Part of her still resisted the idea of getting involved with any man, but she and Duncan were both adult enough to enjoy each other's company without it having to lead to anything serious. They could date until she was reposted. After that she'd have an exciting new place to occupy her, so it was best not to have ties. Why then did the thought of leaving Duncan already hurt a little?

Crazy. She wasn't going to let a man ruin her career when it was only just starting. Men were bad news. They used you and then left you. Her mother had told her that often enough. It was probably the one good piece of advice her mother had given her.

But her head and her heart were not playing on the

29

same team. When she walked into the kitchen the following morning her heart did a crazy jig at the sight of Duncan sitting at the kitchen table, reading a newspaper.

He glanced up and smiled. Against her will, her lips stretched into a wide grin. All of her intentions to play it cool evaporated in the rush of heat between them.

After breakfast he grabbed her hand. "Let me give you the guided tour of Kindrogan."

"What about Holly?"

"Blair will watch Holly. Won't you?" Duncan glanced over his shoulder at his brother, who sat bleary eyed at the kitchen table, knocking back his third cup of coffee.

"Come on, Naomi. We won't be long." Duncan ran up the stairs, tugging her behind him, making her giggle at his quick rundown of the history of the ancient relatives in the portraits.

Then he took her into the bedrooms, showing off the room where Bonnie Prince Charlie was supposed to have spent the night during the march south during the Jacobite rising. "I think this is probably the bed he slept in." Duncan patted the post of an ancient four poster. "It's uncomfortable enough to be that old. We only put guests in here that we really dislike."

In a small gentleman's study, adjacent to the main bedroom in the oldest part of the castle that dated back to the fourteenth century, was a priest hole hidden behind a panel. "One of my forebears, Robert Tavish Mackenzie, spent three weeks in here when the English were searching for him."

Naomi peered into the dark, poky stone cupboard and shivered. "Rather him than me."

They headed up a narrow stairway in a tower and emerged through a low door onto the battlements. The cold air caught in her lungs as tiny flakes of snow spiraled out of the sky and melted against her skin.

Duncan unzipped his thick vest and draped it over

her shoulders to keep her warm, then stood behind her, cuddling her against his body as he pointed out the landmarks: Hew's cottage on the banks of Loch Kinder, the village of Kinder Vale, the Kindrogan Mountain Rescue station and various peaks in the Cairngorms.

"And this is Kindrogan's own little bit of magic, the Heart Stone."

Set into the wall at the top of one of the towers was a reddish piece of rock in among the rough, dark granite. An intricate symbol decorated the face, but it was difficult to make out what the pattern was as it had obviously been weathered over the years.

Naomi snuggled closer to Duncan in the chill, relishing the feel of his strong body against her. "So what's the story behind it?"

"It was reputedly brought back from the crusades by Sir Donald Mackenzie who fought the Moors in Granada in 1248. The story goes that he was homesick for Scotland and his young wife. He walked away from the battle to return home.

"He built the first Kindrogan Castle when he arrived back from Spain. There's very little of the original left, just a few stones in the foundations of the later building. Kindrogan has seen many changes over the centuries.

"This iron-bearing sandstone block is said to be the same type of rock that was used to build the Alhambra Palace. It bears some magical inscription Donald thought would keep his home and family safe. The Mackenzie's who came after him must have given it some credence as they preserved the rock and incorporated it here."

"Wow." Naomi crouched and placed her palm against the chipped old stone. It felt slightly warmer than the granite.

"So, what do you think of Kindrogan?" Duncan asked.

She sensed it was important to him that she liked his home, and she understood why. Duncan was a Mackenzie to his core, very proud of his family history and the castle.

"Fantastic. Like something out of a historical movie or novel, only it's comfortable as well." Kindrogan Castle was definitely a family home with a warm, cozy atmosphere, as if the place knew it was loved and appreciated.

The flakes of snow became huge fluffy puffs that swirled down in dense flurries, obscuring the view. "Time to go inside before we freeze our whatnots off," Duncan said.

They headed back down the narrow steps and finished the tour downstairs. Naomi had already seen most of the ground floor, but Duncan was eager to show her every room, even his office. Journals containing records of the estate's management going back decades filled the shelves.

"These are mine and Hew's, these my father's and these my grandfather's." Duncan ran his fingers along the spines of a shelf full of slender volumes. "In a special climate-controlled storeroom we have record books going back well into the eighteenth century. They make interesting reading."

The boundaries of time faded and a vision of the castle's past stretched before Naomi as if she could see back in history. Duncan did something important here. "You don't really own Kindrogan, do you? You're just passing through."

"It's the principle of stewardship. None of us owns anything. During our lifetimes, we take care of the world for future generations. It's my honor to watch over Kindrogan Estate during my time here." Duncan patted a hand on the door frame affectionately.

Naomi nodded, taking time to digest that. "And your army career?"

"When I joined up as a young doctor, I thought it was the most important thing I'd do in my life. Then my father lost interest in the estate and I took over the administration. In years to come, it's what I do here, at Kindrogan, that will endure."

For a moment, she grasped his sense of purpose, his sense of doing something bigger than himself. But it was a hard concept to visualize and so new to her. So far her life had been dominated by surviving and gaining independence—focusing on herself.

It would take her a while to get used to this idea of stepping back to see the bigger picture. But she wanted to try. Her parents' problem was that they only ever thought of themselves and what they wanted. If everyone had Duncan's philosophy, this world would be a better place.

Naomi sat on one of the old armchairs beside the stove in the kitchen, Holly cuddled in her arms after her breakfast bottle. Duncan hummed to himself as he zapped two bowls of porridge in the microwave.

The kitchen was her favorite room in the house, cozy and reassuring, like a comfort blanket. It was far from modern but everything here was good quality and felt as though it would last forever. The furniture was all heavy, old-fashioned oak, the floor huge polished flagstones, and the cast-iron stove so heavy it would probably need a crane to move it.

Everything in her life had always seemed flimsy and uncertain, as though it could be swept away in an instant, and often had been. This place had a sense of permanence that seeped into her bones. A deep feeling of peace and contentment filled her, one she had never known before and not realized she was missing.

Duncan placed the two bowls of porridge on the table with sugar and milk. Beside them he set down a pot of tea and cups on the scarred wooden surface.

"Breakfast is served. Sorry it's not more exciting. When Mrs. Stewart's not here I live on porridge."

"Looks lovely, Duncan. Thank you." As Naomi rose to place Holly back in her bassinette the phone on the wall by the door rang. Duncan picked it up.

"Hello, Kindrogan Estate...yes, Colonel Mackenzie speaking." He listened for a few seconds and frowned. "We had a heavy snowfall last night. I don't think you should try coming out here today."

Naomi froze, listening closely, a sense of foreboding clenching her gut. "Who was that?" she asked the moment Duncan put down the phone.

"Social Services. The social worker in charge of Holly's case wants to do a home visit to make sure Holly is all right." He glanced out the window at the blanket of whiteness. "She wouldn't be put off. She's probably sitting in a warm office with no clue how much snow we have up here."

"Is she going to take Holly away today?"

"I hope not. I don't want Holly traveling in a car in these conditions. What would happen if it broke down and she was stranded in the cold?"

Emotions flooded through Naomi—outrage, annoyance and concern. But they were all chased away by the fist of pain that tightened around her heart at the thought she might lose Holly today.

"Have they found her mother?"

"I don't think so. My police friend Lyall Stewart would have called me. They just want to check us out. I can see that makes sense, but we're both doctor's. Surely they can trust us with her for a few days? In this weather we should all sit tight until the roads are cleared."

"I know this sounds strange, Duncan, but before the social worker takes Holly, I'd like to give her a bath. Today might be my only chance."

"Let's check with Blair. I know they recommend

newborns aren't bathed too soon." Duncan came and put an arm around her shoulders. "I'm sure we've still got the baby bath we had for Gus. Let me check."

Duncan rootled in the cupboard beside the cloakroom off the kitchen corridor. He returned with a dusty white plastic baby bath and a bottle of baby wash.

Blair wandered in and halted. "Why the grim expressions?"

Duncan told him about the phone call while Naomi circled the kitchen, rocking Holly in her arms, more to soothe herself than the child.

Blair shook his head. "Let's hope the social worker doesn't make it through the snow."

"Is it all right to give Holly a bath?" Naomi asked.

"As long as you're quick and the room's warm," Blair said. "I'd suggest ten minutes max. Newborns lose heat quickly." He eyed the bowls of porridge on the table. "Are you going to eat those?"

"I've lost my appetite," Naomi said.

Duncan grabbed his bowl, sprinkled on some sugar, then downed the contents in a few huge mouthfuls while he was standing. He wiped his mouth on the back of his hand and pointed at the other bowl. "All yours, Blair. We're going to bathe Holly."

"Have fun." Blair sat and poured out a cup of tea.

"Come on," Duncan said to Naomi. "We'll do this in your bathroom where it's nice and warm."

Duncan carried up the bath in one hand and the bassinette in the other, Naomi on his heels with Holly cradled protectively in her arms. A terrible sense of loss hovered, ready to swoop in if she relaxed control of her emotions. She had never been maternal or even thought of having her own baby. How had she grown so attached to Holly in such a short time?

Duncan washed the dust out of the bath, filled it with warm water and tested the temperature before setting it on the bathroom floor. Naomi laid a fluffy towel on the thick mat beside the bath and deposited Holly in the middle, while Duncan uncapped the baby wash and put it where they could reach.

"There you go, little one. You're going to love the warm water." Naomi took off her sweater and rolled up the sleeves of her shirt. Carefully, she undressed the tiny newborn, stroking her thin body affectionately.

Emotion tightened her chest as she picked Holly up and lowered her tiny body into the water. The baby jerked as the liquid touched her, then stilled as Naomi lowered her in. "Is it lovely and warm, poppet?" Naomi's voice cracked and she had to swallow hard.

"All right?" Duncan queried softly.

Naomi nodded, not meeting his gaze. She didn't want him to see the tears in her eyes before she had a chance to blink them away.

Duncan kneeled on the other side of the bath, rolled up his sleeves, and swished some warm water over Holly's chest. "I think she likes it."

"Yes. She's such a sweet little girl, isn't she?" She did not want to part with Holly. It was crazy, it went against all her hopes and dreams, all her plans for the future, but she wanted to keep this little girl.

Squeezing some baby wash into his palm, Duncan gently smoothed it over Holly's skin. He lathered the fluffy blonde hair on the baby's head and rinsed away the bubbles, careful not to get any water or soap in her eyes. This might be the only time they ever bathed her. The next person who did so might not even care about her. Sorrow tightened Naomi's chest.

"I hope they find this little angel's mum and reunite them," Duncan said thoughtfully.

"Why? Her mother's abandoned her. She shouldn't be given a chance to do it again."

Duncan's startled gaze rose to meet hers. She'd shocked him. But he hadn't a clue what he was talking about.

"Surely if Social Services give the woman support—"

"No! Her mother didn't want her." The old anger rose inside Naomi. She lifted Holly from the water, wrapped her in a warm towel and hugged her to her chest, pressing her lips to the baby's hair.

Duncan gaped at her in surprise, then rose and came around the bath. He kneeled and wrapped his arms around both her and Holly. "Were you an abandoned baby, love?"

She shook her head, not trusting her voice. After a moment she answered. "My mum was sixteen when she had me and my father wasn't interested. She didn't abandon me, but I know she didn't want me."

Her earliest memory was of crouching under the table while her mother threw things around the kitchen, screaming at her, "You've ruined my life you little brat." Social workers couldn't keep an eye on at-risk children all the time.

"Naomi love, I'm sorry. I didn't mean to upset you. I'm sure the authorities will do what's best for Holly."

"I wish I could believe that."

"Maybe your mum was too young to understand how to care for you properly, but I'm sure she loved you."

Naomi gave a sad laugh. Duncan was too kind to understand. He wanted to put a good spin on everything. In some ways he was strangely naïve, always believing the best of everyone.

She leaned into him, pressed her face into his neck, breathed in the fragrance of him. Duncan even smelled wholesome, of fresh air and pine forests. She'd never confided in anyone before, never wanted to reveal how her family treated her. She knew the fact they didn't love her was not her fault, but knowing that and believing it were not the same.

"I'm sure Mum didn't love me when I was a child because she doesn't love me now."

Duncan's large hand cradled the back of her head, his fingers stroking her hair, soothing and stimulating at the same time. "Well, your mum might not love you, darling, but I do," he whispered.

Chapter Five

Duncan hadn't meant to reveal his feelings so soon, not here, kneeling on the bathroom floor. He'd imagined declaring his love over a romantic dinner or when snuggled on the sofa in front of the fire one lazy evening. But right now Naomi needed to know that someone loved her. This must be the source of the pain he occasionally saw in her eyes.

He couldn't imagine a mother not loving her child. The children in his family were always cherished. His mother and father might not live at Kindrogan now, but they had both been here when he and his siblings were young and needed them.

"Come on, love. Let's get this little one dried and dressed."

He cupped Naomi's elbow and helped her to her feet with Holly in her arms. She was emotional over the prospect of giving Holly up to the social worker; he'd realized that much. Now he understood why. She must have spent time in the care system herself.

He opened the bathroom door, his arm around Naomi, and they hurried across the cool hallway to the warm bedroom. Naomi laid the baby on the bed and finished drying her before putting on her diaper and sleep suit. It was mid morning, they were expecting the social worker in a few hours, yet all Duncan wanted to do was climb into bed and hold Naomi.

The discordant note of the telephone cut through the silent house like a warning. Naomi glanced up, concern in her eyes. His slight irritation with the social worker had grown to hostility now he knew how upset this whole situation was making Naomi.

"Blair will answer that, but I'll go and check who it is."

Duncan was halfway down the stairs when Blair ambled out of the kitchen hall. "Social worker's not coming now. She says the weather's too bad."

"Common sense wins out after all."

"She said that weather allowing, she'll pick up the baby from the army institute at 9am on January 2nd and take her to a foster home. I thought that would be okay with you, so I said yes."

Duncan had known this would be the plan, yet the thought of Holly being taken to live in a foster home clenched his gut. Foster parents would look after her because they were paid to, but they wouldn't love her.

Some of Naomi's cynicism was rubbing off on him. It sounded as though she knew a whole lot more about the care system in this country than he did, and her experience was not a happy one. As he trod up the stairs, he rubbed the back of his neck, frustrated at his inability to make things right.

Naomi was lying on the bed with Holly wrapped in a blanket, cuddled against her front. She pushed up on an elbow. "Any news?"

"The social worker isn't coming."

Her breath rushed out in obvious relief and she settled back down, gathering Holly close. Duncan sat on the bed behind her and smoothed his hand down her back and over her hip. She was slim but curvy in all the right places—curves that fired his imagination.

He cleared his throat and pulled his mind back to the matter at hand. "The social worker wants to pick

Holly up after the New Year."

Naomi tensed beneath his touch.

He stretched out behind her, head propped on his hand, the other arm curved protectively around her and the baby. "This is the only way it can be. We can't keep Holly, can we? We both have demanding careers."

"I know," she mumbled.

"Your transfer should come through soon and you'll likely be sent overseas. That's something for you to look forward to."

"I'm not sure I want to go now."

Hope flared inside Duncan. Was her new-found reluctance to leave only because of Holly, or did she want to stay with him? Either way she wouldn't have a choice now. She must go where the army posted her.

"We'll be able to visit Holly," he said.

"I'd like that."

"And just because you're being reposted doesn't mean we have to lose contact." He stroked the hair away from her neck and pressed his lips to her skin. "I meant what I said, Naomi. I love you."

She angled her head and peered over her shoulder at him. "Isn't a few days a bit quick to fall in love?"

Duncan laughed—at himself rather than her comment. "I've been in love with you ever since you came to the institute. I couldn't show it, of course. I'm your commanding officer."

"But you're showing it now."

"That's because I don't want to lose you."

Duncan loved her and he didn't want to lose her. Naomi stared at him over her shoulder, her mind blanking, not able to take this in. Nobody had ever loved her. Not her parents or the foster families she'd stayed with. Even the men she'd dated had never said those three little words: "I love you."

A sudden rush of emotion tightened her chest and

41

caught in her throat. She pressed a hand over her mouth. Duncan frowned and stroked the hair back behind her ear. "Naomi love. Are you all right?"

This obviously wasn't the reaction he'd hoped for. "It's just so unexpected." Men were attracted to her. She knew that from the number who asked her out. But they didn't love her. "Are you sure you... how you feel?" She couldn't even bring herself to say the L word.

He laughed, embarrassed to be questioned, she guessed. "Yes." He nodded. "Certain, I'm afraid." He drew in a breath and made to climb off the bed. "Look I've obviously spoken out of turn. I'm sorry."

"No. Don't go." Naomi caught his sleeve, awkwardly twisting so as not to disturb Holly who was fast asleep after her bath.

She'd made him regret his words and that was the last thing she wanted to do. She had no experience with how to handle a declaration of love.

"All right." Duncan sat on the edge of the bed, his eyebrows raised, obviously waiting for her to make the next move.

"Will you put Holly in her bassinette, please?"

"Sure." He leaned across her and scooped the sleeping baby into his arms, smiling down as he carried her across the room to settle her in the baby bed.

He turned, his lips pressed together, uncertainty written in the lines on his forehead. Naomi didn't know what to say in answer to his declaration. She had no idea if she loved Duncan. She had feelings for him, but was it love? The only way she knew to respond was to show him she cared. She rolled over to make more room on the bed and patted the covers. "Come back and lie down."

He did as she asked. She snuggled up close to him, pressing her face against the soft fabric of his shirt, breathing in the fresh, country scent of him. His arms came around her, drawing her closer. His breath warmed her temple a moment before he pressed his lips there.

"I'm attracted to you, Duncan."

"That's a step in the right direction." She heard the self-deprecating humor in his voice and smiled.

"Really attracted. I think about you a lot. At night. In bed."

He chuckled, the sound a deep rumble in his chest under her palm. "Ditto."

Her hand glided over his shoulder, and settled on his side above his belt. His torso was hard with muscle beneath his shirt. She could imagine him picking up a tree trunk and throwing it. She would like to see him toss the caber someday. Even more than that, she'd like to see him without his shirt.

"Naomi, love." His lips trailed tiny kisses down the side of her face onto her neck. "I've dreamed of holding you so many times."

His fingers slid under her shirt onto her back, his touch sending streamers of sensation up her spine.

"We're snowed in and there's nothing to do until Holly wants her next feed," Naomi said.

"So you think we should get to know each other better?"

"Definitely."

"Captain Gray, you have excellent judgment." Then his lips came down on hers and she drifted into the blissful warmth of his embrace.

The next few days passed in a haze of passionate nights and lazy days spent lounging in front of the fire or walking beside the loch in the crisp, white snow.

Duncan borrowed a baby carrier from Hew and strapped Holly on his front. Wrapped in a thick all-in-one suit, she was snuggly and warm while they wandered hand-in-hand, the dogs scampering at their feet.

Duncan showed Naomi the places he'd played as a boy. He described the things he and his brothers and sister had done while they were growing up, all the fun they'd had. It sounded like living in an adventure theme park, so many exciting activities to do right on their doorstep.

She and Duncan built a small snowman—her first ever—and snapped photos on their phones of themselves standing beside it. Naomi took photos and videos of Holly in her bassinette, in the bath, awake, asleep, sticking out her tongue, yawning and sneezing. She wanted to capture every possible moment as a record to view later, once Holly was taken away.

Just the thought of losing the baby was enough to bring tears to her eyes so she tried not to think about it. For the few days between Christmas and The New Year, she lived in a perfect world where only she, Duncan and Holly existed, in the fantasy world of Kindrogan Castle.

Probably sensing they wanted time alone together, Blair went to visit with Megan and Daniel or Hew and Fergus. But it couldn't last forever. On December 31st, Duncan and Blair had to go to London for the Royal Army Medical Corps New Year's Eve Ball.

Naomi stood in the entrance hall with her arms wrapped around Duncan, her ear pressed to his chest, listening to his steady heartbeat, counting down the seconds until he left. "I wish you didn't have to go."

"I wouldn't unless it was important." He glanced up the stairs, looking for Blair who had yet to come down. "The ball is to raise money for the Heroes' Kids charity that Blair's involved with, for the children of servicemen who lost their lives."

"I know." Blair had talked about the charity and it was obviously important to him. Naomi stood on tiptoe and kissed Duncan's lips. "You'll be back tomorrow?"

"I promise. We'll have one more night together with

Holly before the social worker picks her up and we have to return to work."

Work seemed like a distant memory. Like something Naomi had done in another lifetime. But it had only been a week since Duncan brought her here from the institute. How would she maintain a professional distance from him at the institute now that they were close?

"You're sure you'll be all right here on your own with Holly?" he asked.

"Of course. I know where everything is. You go and enjoy yourself."

Duncan pulled a face then drew her closer. "I'd have far more fun if you were coming with me."

They'd discussed this. She'd love to go but one of them had to stay with Holly and that was her. Anyway, she wanted to spend as much time as possible with the darling little girl before they gave her up.

Blair bounded down the stairs, a bag in one hand and a suit cover in the other. "Well, I won't be back now before I return to Africa. It was lovely to meet you, Naomi. I hope to see you again." He kissed her cheek.

They headed into the kitchen. Blair went out the back door and tossed his bags in the back of the Land Rover. The chains were permanently on the tires at this time of year, and the engine was already running, warming up the vehicle before they set off in the snow.

Duncan put his bags in with Blair's as Naomi watched from the doorway, her arms wrapped around her middle against the cold. He came back and hugged her tightly, kissing her. He leaned his forehead against hers. "I'll see you late tomorrow. Wait up for me, won't you."

"Of course."

With a sigh, he headed for the Land Rover. He climbed in, shifted it into gear with a nasty grating sound, and pulled away.

Naomi shut the back door and dashed through the house to the window in the dining room that gave a good view out of the front. She watched Duncan's vehicle trundle through the snow on the narrow road around the lake until it disappeared from sight.

He was gone. She had the whole castle to herself. She had Holly to herself. Even as she missed Duncan, the prospect of being solely responsible for the baby filled her with a strange sense of excitement. How she had changed in a week. On Christmas day, she'd been horrified to find herself responsible for a baby; today she couldn't think of anything in the world she'd rather do.

A few weeks ago, if someone had told Naomi that she would not only be left in charge of a newborn baby but also a castle, she would have panicked. Yet the reality was not nearly as scary as it sounded.

Kindrogan was like any other house, only on a slightly larger scale, and with towers and battlements. As long as there wasn't a power outage and the boiler kept working, she would be just fine.

Duncan had piled a supply of logs next to the fireplace in the drawing room and there was food in the pantry. All she had to do was relax and enjoy her last two days with Holly.

She put Holly in the baby carrier, strapped it on her chest and roamed the castle. Retracing the route Duncan had taken when he'd shown her around, she remembered the stories of his family, his deep voice and his easy smile. Her heart contracted with wanting him, wishing he were here with her instead of in London.

She went into his bedroom and laid a hand on the comforter, imagining him lying here every night alone. Was he lonely? The thought pinched her heart. She hated to think of him being unhappy.

"Let's lie on Duncan's bed shall we, little one?" Naomi smiled down at Holly, and kissed one of her tiny fists. Careful not to crush the baby, she backed onto the bed, and stretched out where Duncan normally lay every night, her head on his pillow, Holly lying on her chest in the baby carrier.

Duncan has spent the last few nights with her, but they had always slept in her bedroom, not his. Apart from the tour, this was the first time she'd visited his room. She stared out of the window, taking in the view of Loch Kinder, imagining Duncan doing the same thing.

Photos of his family rested on the top of a solid old chest of drawers, including a picture of his mother and father. They might not be here, but they were obviously very important to him.

After a while, she continued the tour, taking the steps up the tower to the battlements carefully, aware of the precious little person strapped to her chest.

The clouds had cleared, leaving a bright blue sky, the sun sparkling off the white landscape. The pine trees wore thick, snowy cloaks, and spiders' webs of ice fringed the water's edge on Loch Kinder. How had she ever thought Scotland was dull and boring? Now she saw it through Duncan's eyes, she thought it was ancient and beautiful. A bit colder and wetter than she'd like, but still, you couldn't have everything.

She stayed outside only a few minutes, afraid Holly might get cold. As she walked back towards the tower a small red stone bounced off her shoe. She stooped to pick it up. The corner of the Heart Stone had chipped off. From the look of the cracked and chipped old stone, bit's fell off frequently.

Naomi straightened, the chip resting on her palm. She dropped it in her pocket, intending to give it to Duncan when he returned. The stone was symbolic of everything that Kindrogan meant to him, his heritage, his family and his place in history. He would certainly want to preserve even a tiny piece of such a thing.

Or maybe she would keep this chip of the Heart Stone as a memento, something to remind her of Duncan and Kindrogan when she was posted overseas.

Chapter Six

Today was nearly the worst day of Duncan's life. The day his mother had left Kindrogan for good just topped it, but not by much. He drove the Land Rover away from Kindrogan Castle, Holly strapped in the borrowed baby car seat in the back, Naomi at his side.

After such a wonderful week with Naomi and Holly, this felt even worse in contrast. They had one last night all together at Kindrogan when he arrived back from London, and he'd made the most of it. He'd held Naomi in his arms as she slept, and took his turn to feed Holly for a final time. But this morning everything changed.

Every mile they traveled, Naomi hunched tighter in on herself, her face a mask of misery. She was devastated to be losing Holly and Duncan felt nearly as bad, although he hid it better. He had to.

He reached for her hand and squeezed her cold, stiff fingers. "She'll be all right, love." The words were all he could come up with to comfort her and they weren't much help.

She glanced at him, tears in her eyes. If only he could take her in his arms and make everything better, but life didn't work like that. Not in this situation, anyway.

He drove up the army institute access road and turned in beside the square gray accommodation block.

"I suggest you say goodbye to Holly here. Take some time to change into uniform. Come over later, when you feel better."

She nodded. "I want to get in the back of the car with her for a few minutes."

"Okay. You do that, love."

Naomi climbed out and slid into the back beside Holly's baby seat. Duncan watched in the rear-view mirror as she laid her cheek against the baby's hair, and touched her tiny hands and feet. "I'll miss you, poppet," she whispered.

Tears pricked the back of Duncan's eyes. He glanced away, fingers clenched around the steering wheel, and focused on something else. A delivery van trundled up the road and turned into the army hospital. He tried to guess what it was delivering to help him regain control.

He tuned out Naomi's whispered words, but his gaze slid back to the mirror in time to see her kiss Holly's cheek. She wiped her eyes with the side of her hand and drew in a breath.

"Thanks for the ride, Duncan. I'll see you later." Naomi opened the back door and jumped out.

He climbed out to grab her bag from the back. Pulling her into his arms, he held her tight. He wanted to tell her she'd get over this and move on, that she just had to give it time. But this wasn't what she wanted to hear right now. "No hurry. We can manage without you today if necessary."

He released her and she headed for the accommodation block. Swiping her security pass, she unlocked the door and went inside.

Duncan's heart felt like a lump of granite in his chest as he climbed back in the vehicle. His gaze was drawn over his shoulder. For once Holly was wide awake. Her bright blue eyes seemed to be focused on his face, but he had no idea if she could see him clearly. Even if she could, she wouldn't remember him.

"Heck," he growled at himself as he slid the vehicle into gear. He didn't have time to be sentimental. Most of the patients who'd gone home for Christmas were due to return today. He had a hospital to run. He took the access road to the main institute building, and pulled up in his parking space by the front entrance.

As he stopped, a middle-aged woman with glasses climbed out of a small red hatchback parked nearby. "Colonel Mackenzie?" She held out a hand and he shook it. "I'm Jenny Hopper from social services."

"You're prompt, Ms. Hopper."

"I thought it was best to sort things out early. Is the baby in your car?" She eyed the Land Rover with a frown.

"Yes, in the back, in a car seat. We've taken good care of her, Ms. Hopper. And her name's Holly, by the way."

She nodded. "I can't see any problem with calling her that. I'll make sure to change it on the paperwork."

Duncan opened his rear door and the social worker unclipped Holly from her seat and lifted her out. "You're one bonny wee lassie, aren't you, Holly. It looks as though you've cared for her well, Colonel. Thank you very much."

She smiled and seemed to be a nice woman. Duncan watched as she strapped Holly in the car seat in the back of her small car. He grabbed the bag of Holly's things, a few clothes, the bottle, and some diapers, and offered it.

"On no, Colonel Mackenzie. Not necessary, thank you. We supply a baby starter pack to our foster families. You keep those."

Duncan looked at the bag in his hand. He wished she'd take the things. He didn't want Naomi to see them. It would only upset her.

"Well, I'll be on my way." Jenny Hopper climbed in her car and started the engine.

Duncan knocked on the driver's window. "Will my girlfriend and I be able to visit her?"

The social worker's eyebrows rose in thought. "I don't see why not."

"Will you ask the foster parents to contact me when she's settled in? I want to go and meet them." And make sure they pass muster. He would have no hesitation in complaining if he didn't think they were suitable. He pulled a Kindrogan Estates business card from his pocket, one with a photograph of the castle on the front and his name, rank, and phone number on the back.

She examined the photograph for a moment, her gaze rising to him, curiously. "Is this where you live?"

"My father is Sir Robert Mackenzie, the local laird." He rarely flaunted his family connections, preferring to be judged on his own merit. But right now he wanted to score all the points he could. He wanted this woman to understand she was dealing with someone who had influence.

"I see, well, Holly won't be staying anywhere quite this grand, but I hope she'll be comfortable."

She'd better be, Duncan thought as the woman backed up and drove out of the car park. Or he'd want to know the reason why. He was going to keep close tabs on what happened to Holly.

The small red hatchback disappeared around a bend. Duncan's rigid hold on his feelings wavered and he clenched his fist against his thigh. He couldn't be emotional; he had a position of authority to maintain and a hospital to run.

His gaze flitted over the hospital laundry to the top of the accommodation block. He swallowed hard at the thought of Naomi there alone, desperately upset. This relationship was going to make working together difficult, exactly why he had kept his feelings for her to himself for so long.

As he paced inside, he wondered if it might actually be a good thing she was about to be reposted.

"Good morning, sir."

He nodded to the nurse who greeted him.

"Good morning, Colonel. I hope you had a lovely Christmas." The civilian receptionist there to handle the non-military patients greeted him as he walked past.

"Very good, thank you." He smiled, even though it was the last thing he felt like doing. He had never imagined that parting with one tiny baby could make him feel this bad.

He rubbed a hand over his face as he entered the sanctuary of his office and closed the door behind him. The best thing to do was throw himself into his research. He had an important medical trial underway, assessing potential treatments for non-freezing cold injuries, a health problem that mainly affected military personnel.

He leafed through the mail that had been opened and laid on his desk. One letter caught his eye and he pulled it out; Naomi's new posting. His gaze scanned the page and he groaned. The army was sending her to Africa.

He cursed under his breath and dropped into his seat. According to Blair, conditions in the field hospital there were grim. It was dangerous as well. He did *not* want Naomi in that place, but it was out of his hands.

He groaned again when he noticed she was due to fly out from RAF Brize Norton in Oxfordshire the following day. This letter must have been sitting in the mail room since before Christmas. She'd need to get on a train today if she were to make it in time. The only good thing about this was that Blair would be on that flight. He could keep an eye on her.

Duncan called Naomi's mobile phone. When he got no answer, he decided to walk across to her apartment.

This was something he wanted to discuss with her in private.

Naomi sluiced cold water on her face and patted her red eyes with a towel. As she glanced up at the bathroom mirror, her breath hissed out in a sigh. She looked a mess. She did *not* want Duncan to see her like this, yet she needed to go to work to take her mind off Holly.

Moping around in her room all day would do her no good at all. She grabbed a brush and stroked it vigorously through her messy hair before tying the strands back in a ponytail.

Scotland had won her heart during her week at Kindrogan, but she would never like her horrible army accommodations. The room was more like a cell than an apartment, just a tiny bedsit with a minuscule kitchen and a bathroom—and always cold.

She changed into uniform before dabbing some concealer around her eyes, to hide the redness, and adding a touch of mascara.

As she laced up her boots the entry buzzer sounded. She opened the door to find Duncan standing outside. His grim expression sent a shock of concern through her. "Is something wrong with Holly?"

"No." He shook his head. "She's fine. The social worker collected her. She seemed like a reasonable woman."

Naomi breathed through her mouth, stifling the tears that threatened again. She had to get over this sense of loss and move on. Holly was not hers and never would be. Duncan stepped forward and settled his hands at her waist. His uniform accentuated his height and solid build. She flattened her palms on his chest, an illicit thrill zipping through her to be touching him while they were on duty.

He drew her close and kissed her. "How are you

holding up, love?"

"I miss Holly. I'll never forget her, but I'll survive."

He cradled her cheek in his hand and kissed her temple. "Your new posting came through. The notification must have arrived before Christmas."

"Where?"

"Africa."

"Yes!" She bounced on her toes, a shot of excitement energizing her. This was her dream, to travel to exotic places and experience other cultures. This was the main reason she'd joined the army.

"You'll stay in touch, won't you?" he said.

Her enthusiasm faded as she remembered this meant leaving Duncan. "Of course. But I think this is what I need. Everything here will remind me of Holly. I can't handle that right now."

Glancing down, he straightened her collar, his fingers brushing her neck. "It might be for the best. I'll struggle to keep my hands off you all day if you stay. That won't do anything for my professional reputation."

"Ditto." She ran her hands up over his shoulders and pressed her face against him, breathing in his fresh, country smell, remembering the nights in his arms at Kindrogan. She would miss him so much. But she needed to get away. "When do I leave?"

"You fly out from Brize Norton tomorrow. We need to put you straight on a train south."

"Gosh." Naomi glanced around her room at her possessions.

"I'll take your things to Kindrogan and store them if you like."

"That'll be great. Thanks."

"It means you'll have to come back to me." He gave a self-deprecating smile.

She smacked him playfully on the arm. "Of course I'll come back to you."

"Will you?" The note of uncertainty in his voice tugged at her heart.

"Yes." She rose on her toes to kiss him. She cared deeply for this man. If only she could say the words he wanted to hear, but she wasn't certain that what she felt was love. "You're special to me, Duncan."

"Yes. Of course." His mouth firmed and he stepped back, his demeanor changing to that of her commanding officer. "Africa is about as tough as it gets, Naomi. The field hospital there handles a steady stream of seriously injured soldiers. You asked for a transfer and this is the army throwing you in at the deep end to see if you can swim."

"Don't worry about me. I'll swim." And Africa would be lovely and warm. She couldn't wait to get away from cold, wet Britain.

"Meet Lt. Col. Cameron Knight," Blair said, extending a hand towards the tall, dark-haired man who was issuing orders to the soldiers carrying equipment up the ramp into the belly of the army aircraft. "He's in command of the army's critical care, air-support team."

"Pleased to meet you, sir," Naomi said, saluting.

Lieutenant Colonel Knight held out his hand with a friendly grin and she shook it. "Welcome aboard, Captain Gray. I hope we have an uneventful flight. We're carrying a lot of equipment over to Africa, so you'll have to squeeze in between the crates, I'm afraid. This flight, we're a freight service on the way out and a hospital plane on the way back."

His gaze skipped over her shoulder. "Mind your backs." She and Blair stepped aside as two soldiers carried in a folded bed, stowed it against the side of the plane, and strapped it in securely.

"We've nearly finished loading. I suggest you head to the seating area and stow your bags. Talk to you later."

Blair grabbed his bag and Naomi's and carried them

up the metal ramp. They headed along a narrow corridor that had been left between the containers of equipment.

Naomi angled her head, reading the markup on the crates. They were carrying medicines, sterile surgical equipment, bedding, electrical equipment for the OR, and other medical supplies. "What's all this for? I thought the field hospital outside Rejerrah was already equipped."

"The rebels intensified their bombardment of the area just before Christmas. I believe some of the equipment was damaged."

"Oh." The simmering excitement in her stomach faded at the thought of the field hospital being attacked. Although Africa was a conflict zone, she hadn't thought the medical staff was in danger.

Blair stowed their bags behind the seats then sat, leaving room for her to do the same. She settled and fastened the lap belt for takeoff. With the loading door open it was chilly and she shivered.

The small passenger area was boxed in by all the crates and there were no windows. It was a little claustrophobic. To distract herself, she pulled her phone from her pocket and checked for messages. Duncan had texted her the previous evening to ask if she had arrived safely. But there was nothing from him today.

At the thought of Duncan, her stomach clenched with a sick sense that something was not right. He'd dropped her at the train station yesterday afternoon and arranged for Blair to meet her in Oxford. They'd hugged and kissed when he said goodbye, but his usual smile faded behind his professional face as he waved her off. It was as if he had withdrawn from her.

She wished they'd had a chance to have a heart-to-heart discussion, so she could explain her confusion over how she felt. But they hadn't done that. Or she hadn't. She couldn't blame Duncan. He'd laid his feelings on the line. She was the one who'd stayed quiet.

"Penny for them," Blair said.

"Oh, nothing." Naomi shrugged. She couldn't discuss her feelings for Duncan with his brother. That seemed disloyal.

"You'll need to switch that off for takeoff." Blair nodded at her phone.

"Right." She quickly tapped out a text. "Just boarded. Ready to take off. I miss you. xxx Naomi." She hit send and made sure the text went before she switched off her phone.

The scraping and banging of cargo being loaded stopped and Lieutenant Colonel Knight appeared between the crates with four other soldiers and took the spare seats. "Take off in ten minutes," he said.

He joked with his men, and Blair joined in, obviously good friends with Cameron.

"So how's the Heroes' Kids Fund going, Blair? You raised a tidy sum on New Year's Eve."

"Very well. We're finalizing the kids' vacation schedule for this year. I'm hoping to host a group at Kindrogan just before Christmas."

"So will you dress up as Santa Claus?" Cameron asked with a grin.

"Not sure a white beard will suit me."

The roar of the engines increased, making it difficult to hear each other. Naomi rested her head back as the plane took off. She normally liked to look out the window when she flew. It was unnerving being unable to see outside.

"Time for some shuteye." Blair wedged a small pillow behind his head.

"I find it difficult to sleep on a plane," she said.

"You'll soon learn to take power naps anywhere. It's a necessity for army doctors. There're no comfortable on-call rooms in a field hospital. I've seen surgeons sit down on the OR floor and nap between surgeries when it's at its busiest."

"I've done that," Cameron chipped in. "I was operating thirty-six hours straight once. I had to stop and catch a couple of naps because my eyes were so tired I couldn't see anymore."

Naomi stared at him incredulously. "You don't believe me," he said with a wry laugh. "You wait and see."

She glanced at Blair for his reaction, but he had closed his eyes. She'd worked the usual rotation of specialties that every young doctor did while training. She'd even spent a couple of months at the huge military hospital at Brize Norton. She'd often been on call for twenty-four hours and occasionally thirty-six, but that was rarely non-stop work.

She couldn't even visualize a situation where a surgeon operated for thirty-six hours and slept on the OR floor. Lieutenant Colonel Knight must be pulling her leg. This was probably a joke the experienced officers played on the newbies.

Chapter Seven

"Do come in, Colonel Mackenzie," Mrs. O'Brien, Holly's foster mother, said.

Duncan stepped inside the terraced house, ducking beneath the top of the doorframe. It was an old miner's cottage built a few hundred years ago, and men must have been shorter then.

The friendly elderly woman led him through to a front room with a gas fire burning behind a fireguard. Music blared, and three preschoolers dashed around the room, shouting and throwing toys about. Duncan winced at the mayhem, but Mrs. O'Brien seemed oblivious. She had probably gone deaf long ago.

A distressed screech issued from the bassinette set on a dining table squashed in the space behind the sofa at the end of the room. "There she goes again." Mrs. O'Brien raised her eyes to the ceiling as if seeking celestial guidance. "What a fussy baby Holly is, always crying."

"Not while we had her," Duncan mumbled. He dodged the lively children and leaned over the bassinette, his heart jumping at the sight of Holly. Her little face was red, her eyes wet with tears, her tiny fists clenched. The poor little soul was probably scared out of her wits by the racket. At Kindrogan she'd got used to peace and quiet. No wonder she wasn't settled.

Duncan lifted her into his arms and rocked her, soothing her as he'd done in the past.

"Can we go somewhere quieter?"

"What?" Mrs. O'Brien said.

"Somewhere quieter," he repeated slowly so she could read his lips.

Duncan rubbed Holly's back, her tiny head under his chin as he followed the woman through to the kitchen.

They both squeezed into the tiny room and Duncan closed the door with his foot to shut out the noise.

"I gather you found the poor little thing outside your army hospital," Mrs. O'Brien said.

"Yes. She spent her first week with me. She slept very well. We hardly heard a peep out of her except when she was hungry."

"That's a mystery, then. She's not sleeping well at all now."

"Maybe she needs a quieter room."

"Oh, no, Colonel. Babies enjoy listening to other children. It makes them feel part of a family. I've been fostering children for thirty years. I've never met a baby who didn't like the sound of other children playing."

Well, you've met one now, Duncan thought. He glanced around the kitchen. It was clean, and Mrs. O'Brien seemed nice, but she appeared to have little control over the three preschoolers. This house seemed too small to contain so many energetic youngsters. Children needed space to run and play, space like he had at Kindrogan.

Not everyone was that lucky. But there was a park just down the road. The kids still screaming in the next room needed to run off some of their surplus energy there.

He cradled the back of Holly's head in his hand and stared down at her wrinkled red face. She was hot and sweaty because she'd worked herself into such a state. He'd not seen her like this before.

She wasn't happy here. This was not what he wanted for her. She deserved parents who loved her and paid attention to her needs.

Raising her, he pressed a kiss to her forehead. He'd been in turmoil over the last forty-eight hours. Losing both Holly and Naomi on the same day had knocked him sideways. He had no influence over whether Naomi came back to him or not. She didn't love him, so he suspected he'd lose her and any chance of the children he longed for.

He already loved Holly so it made perfect sense for him to offer her a home. He wanted to look after this baby girl, to be there for her when she needed him, and show her the beauty of this wonderful country they lived in.

The adoption services website said single people could adopt children. That was what he planned to do.

Torrential rain poured off the fuselage of the army aeromed plane, forming a sheet of water barring Naomi's path. She stood beside Blair in the dry, on the lowered ramp of the aircraft, squinting to see through the deluge.

"I didn't expect it to be raining like this when we arrived in Africa." This made the Scottish rain seem like a light shower.

"It shouldn't be raining in January. It's supposed to be the dry season," Blair said. "Must be something to do with global warming."

A jeep pulled up close by. A soldier climbed out of the driver's seat and dashed under cover with them. "Evening, doc," he said, saluting Blair.

"Corporal Webster, this is Captain Gray," Blair said, introducing her. "Another doctor."

The man smiled. "Hope you had a reasonable trip, ma'am. We've got some lovely weather to greet you." The man picked up her bag. "If you're ready, I'll take you over to the hospital, ma'am, sir."

"Lead the way, Webster," Blair said. The corporal dashed through the rain sluicing down off the plane, and headed for his vehicle.

Blair followed him, Naomi on his heels. Rain poured over her hair, ran down her face, and soaked her to the skin in a matter of seconds. By the time she jumped into the back of the sandy-colored Jeep, her army uniform was so wet she could have rung it out.

"Oh, heck." She blinked the water from her eyes and wiped her face with her hands. "I didn't know it was possible for rain to come down this heavily."

Despite the rain it was hot. The inside of the vehicle steamed up, the windows fogging as if they were in a sauna. Naomi's skin prickled with sweat and she wished she could take off her army shirt and just wear the tank top she had on underneath.

The Jeep moved slowly, Corporal Webster squinting through the windshield, the wipers unable to keep it clear. A dark metal carcass loomed out of the murk like the bones of a dinosaur. Naomi craned her neck around as they passed.

"That's an Apache helicopter that was shelled just before Christmas. The rebels often bombard the airfield at night. They deploy mobile rocket launchers on the backs of trucks. They park up somewhere out there in the desert, fire for ten or fifteen minutes then disappear into the sand dunes before the NATO patrols reach them."

Naomi's heart thudded, her nerves on edge. She knew this posting was in a NATO theatre of operations, an active conflict zone, but she hadn't expected to be anywhere near the fighting. Everything she'd read said army doctors were never hurt.

The Jeep bumped through potholes and over rubble then pulled up outside a cement-block building. Blair jumped out, grabbing both their bags before he ran inside. She followed, getting another drenching on the way. Her carefully styled hair came out of its fixing and stuck to her face in rat's tails.

She was soaked, her bag was soaked, and probably everything inside it was also soaked. What a way to arrive at her new posting.

As she tidied her hair, a skinny man in scrubs came towards them with an unlit cigarette hanging out of his mouth.

"Have a good Christmas, Bourne?" Blair said.

"You're joking aren't you? Short staffed, and constant bombardment. This place is Hell on earth."

"Major Bourne is one of the surgeons," Blair said. "This is Naomi Gray, the new anesthetist."

The man's gaze passed over her without interest. "Why do they keep sending these greenhorns?"

"Everyone has to learn."

"Not in my operating room, thank you very much." The man shouldered past them and strode outside.

"Don't take offense. Bourne's been here too long and he's burned out. Your direct superior will be Major Julia Braithwaite. You'll like her. Let's see if she's around."

Naomi followed Blair down the cement corridor. Naked light bulbs hung at intervals, and bunches of cables ran along the ceiling. The plaster on the walls was cracked and had fallen off in places.

"OR one," Blair said, pointing at a door guarded by a plastic strip curtain. "OR two is just down the hall."

Naomi tucked a finger around one of the plastic strips and pushed it aside. Inside, the floor and walls were covered in plastic sheet. An operating table stood in the middle of the room with the usual equipment arranged around it.

"It's a challenge to maintain a sterile environment here, but we do our best."

She had never seen anything like this before. It was

going to be different, that was for sure.

"This used to be the offices of an airfreight company. It's convenient for us. The NATO forces are housed in the buildings around the airfield. We go over there to the mess sometimes, other times we exist on ration packs in here." He pushed open the door to a small room with a table in the middle and a few chairs around it. A coffee machine and electric kettle sat on a side table beside a stack of ration packs.

A short woman with curly dark hair came out of a room, and grinned at them. "Blair, my darling, how was your Christmas?"

"Wonderful, thanks, Julia." He touched Naomi's shoulder. "This is your new anesthetist." Julia extended a hand and they shook. "Great to meet you. I'll show you to your room and you can settle in while it's quiet. We have to take advantage of times like this."

"I'll leave you to it, then." Blair smiled at Naomi. "I spend most of my time at the refugee camp coordinating with the charity workers who specialize in child care, but I'll look you up next time I'm back."

"Thank you, Blair. I really appreciate your help." She would have been lost without him. So much for being independent.

She picked up her bag and walked along the corridor a few steps behind Julia. They turned into a more dilapidated part of the building. Old air-conditioning units hummed in the corridor. The lights were on here and the rooms had no doors, only curtains hanging over the doorways.

"This part of the building is under the hill. We have our rooms here as it gives us better protection. Bathroom's at the end. Nothing special I'm afraid, but we manage." She stopped and pulled aside a door curtain. "You can bed down here. I've put some gear in there for you."

Naomi poked her head inside. It was pitch black.

"No windows?"

"Not under the hill." Julia bent and switched on a table lamp standing on a chair beside the door. "You won't need much light. You won't be in here very often."

"Oh, okay." Naomi stared at the shadowy room, shocked by how basic it was.

Julia pointed at a sheet of canvas stretched over a metal frame with a sleeping bag and a small pillow on top of it. "Make yourself comfortable."

Naomi stepped in, reluctantly. She wasn't keen on enclosed, dark places. She was a little claustrophobic, but she didn't complain. Having asked for this transfer, she would make the best of things and learn all she could.

Dropping her bag on the ground, she pulled her phone out of her pocket.

"No mobile phone reception in here, of course. You have to walk to the top of the hill for that. But I wouldn't bother in this weather. You'd probably ruin your phone."

Naomi's heart plummeted. She wanted to check if Duncan had replied to her text and tell him she'd arrived safely.

"Hungry?" Julia asked.

"Not really. I had something on the flight." And her appetite had deserted her.

"Okay. I would dry off and get some shuteye while you can. We sleep when it's quiet, whether it's the day or night. Life doesn't follow normal rules here. We make it up as we go along." She laughed as though she'd made a joke.

"If the rebels shell the airfield tonight we might be busy, although they've been quiet since the rain started."

"Okay. Thanks."

"Sleep well."

With that, Major Braithwaite pulled the curtain closed. As her footsteps retreated along the corridor, Naomi stared at the ragged red damask that must once have been a beautiful curtain, hanging at a window somewhere.

She gazed around her tiny black hole of a room with a burgeoning sense of horror. Her apartment in Scotland had been luxurious compared to this.

Sitting on the canvas bed, she unlaced her boots, and pulled off her sodden socks. Grit prickled the soles of her bare feet as she moved around the room, sorting out her clothes, hanging them up to dry as best she could. This room was no better than the priest hole at Kindrogan.

Once she had taken off her wet clothes and dressed in a dry top and panties, she lay on the sleeping bag, and looked through the photos on her phone. Imagining sweet little Holly in her arms made her sigh, but she found herself scrolling past the endless baby photos to find some of Duncan. At the sight of his laughing face, as he stood beside the snow man they'd built, longing tugged painfully at her heart.

Losing Holly had upset her so much it overwhelmed her. Only now did she realize how much she missed Duncan; how much she wanted to feel his arms around her.

Why on earth had she been in such a hurry to leave him?

It rained, and rained, and rained. Naomi was either soaked from the rain or soaked with sweat in the sticky heat. She could barely breathe for the humidity, and spots of mold grew on everything, her clothes, her boots, and her bedding.

Everyone kept saying that it was the dry season, and it shouldn't be raining. But it didn't stop. The one good thing was that the deluge made it impossible for the conflict to continue. The rebel forces were quiet, the Apache helicopters grounded, and the NATO patrols sat it out at base.

Once the medical staff had unpacked and set up the new equipment that had arrived on Naomi's flight, there was little for them to do. They whiled away the hours in the mess hall, with the soldiers, or lounged under the shelter of the porch at the door to the field hospital.

Naomi got into a strange routine, waking when she wanted to, and dressing in shorts and a tank top, with nothing to do but wait for the fighting that would start again when the rain stopped. The endless drumming of raindrops was like white noise. After a few days, she grew so used to it she barely noticed anymore.

She wandered out of the hospital door and dropped down on a chair beside Julia Braithwaite a few yards from the endless sheet of water falling from the sky. Most of the other doctors, nurses, and medical technicians sat on the row of plastic chairs, chatting, reading books, or staring at their mobile phones, waiting for the elusive few bars of reception to flash up on the screen long enough for a text to be sent or received.

Naomi texted Duncan, and asked about Holly, Kindrogan, and the army institute, waiting hours for each reply. She chatted to Julia about her posting in Scotland, each day revealing more details until she finally confided her feelings for Duncan, and described her week at Kindrogan.

"You must have been sick as a parrot when you were posted here," Julia said. "No one would want to leave a jammy posting like Scotland, especially when the Colonel sounds like such a sweetheart."

"Yeah," Naomi mumbled. She didn't admit that she'd asked for the transfer. Julia would think she was crazy. She thought she was crazy.

Naomi stared at her phone screen, at Duncan's latest message. "Visited Holly and she seems fine."

If she'd stayed in Scotland she could have visited Holly. She ran her fingers back through her limp, sweaty hair and sighed. Whoever said that you don't know what you've got until it's gone was right. What an idiot she'd been.

She needed to talk to Duncan. She had something to say that was too important to put in a text. But the rain was relentless.

On the fifth day in Africa she texted the words she longed to say to him out loud. "I love you, Duncan. I'm sorry I didn't tell you before I left. I was a fool."

For nearly two hours she sat staring at her phone screen, waiting for a reply, the rain pounding the cement a few yards away. Finally, her phone dinged to signal receipt of a text. With a tripping heart, she tapped in her password to read it.

"I love you too. I'll be waiting for you when you want to come home."

"Home," she whispered to herself. She had only spent one week at Kindrogan, but it felt more like home than anywhere she had ever lived. She dug in the pocket of her shorts, pulled out the tiny piece of the Heart Stone from Kindrogan Castle, and cradled it in her palm.

It wasn't just the place that made Kindrogan welcoming, it was Duncan. He was the true heart of the castle. Wherever Duncan was would be home to her.

Chapter Eight

Finally, after two weeks, Naomi was greeted by an eerie silence as she headed along the hospital corridor. She shouldered open the exit door to find bright blue sky, the sun blasting heat down.

She gazed around curiously. She had only seen this place through the lens of falling drips. Now she could see it clearly. Tumbledown cement buildings with collapsed roofs and teetering walls ringed the yard outside the field hospital. Huge potholes full of dirty water, piles of rubble, and heaps of trash lay all around.

Julia came out of the door behind her. "Hallelujah! The rain's stopped. Want to walk over to the mess?" Across the airfield troops were out and about, a group kicking a soccer ball around, some sitting on lumps of rock smoking, others in overalls working on the Apache helicopters.

"Later," Naomi said. "First I want to climb up the hill and call Duncan."

"Okay, I'll show you the way."

They scrambled up a furrow that the water had worn between the rocks. Flies buzzed at Naomi's face and she batted them away. The unfamiliar sun beat down on her head, almost unbearably hot. At least they would be able to dry things outside now.

When they reached the top, Naomi put her hands on

her hips and scanned the view, seeing her surroundings for the first time. The devastated city of Rejerrah lay below. Some of the areas were nothing but heaps of rubble; other buildings had gaping holes in the sides. Rivers of rain ran along the streets. People crossed on planks laid over the rushing water.

She wrinkled her nose. "What is that stink?"

"A combination of smog and sewage."

"Agh." Naomi pressed a hand over her nose as she turned to look out across what had once been a desert but was now a sea of waterlogged dirt, sprouting weeds. In the distance, a shanty town of tents and cabins lay on the horizon amid a rough landscape covered with rocks and scrubby bushes.

Julia raised an arm and pointed. "That's the refugee camp."

"Where Blair works." How had he coped with the rain, under canvas, out there in the middle of nowhere?

Naomi's gaze wandered the alien landscape, a sense of unreality making it difficult to take in. "This looks like a scene from a dystopian movie."

"Certainly dystopia, but very much real." As if to underline Julia's words, a huge boom sounded in the city. A plume of smoke billowed up as one side of a building collapsed.

Naomi's hand went to her thudding heart.

"Looks like the rebels are targeting the financial district. They didn't waste any time getting started again."

A shout from below drew their attention. "You're needed in the OR."

"Here we go," Julia said. "I think we've just had the calm before the storm. You make your call then come down. Best if you shadow me for the first few ops to familiarize you with our procedures."

"Okay, thanks. I'll be as quick as I can."

As Julia scrambled down the hill, Naomi sat on a

rock, pulled out her phone, and speed-dialed Duncan's number, praying he would pick up.

"Naomi." She heard the smile in Duncan's voice as he answered.

"It's stopped raining. I'm up on the hill above the field hospital. It's the only place I can get enough signal to call you."

"Are you all right?"

She glanced at the plume of smoke rising from the recent explosion, and hesitated a moment before answering. "Yes."

"I miss you, love."

"I miss you too, Duncan. I'm so sorry I didn't tell you that I love you before I left. I was confused."

"It doesn't matter. I just want you back here with me, safe and sound."

"I wish I'd never put in for a transfer."

"Do you want to come home?"

Naomi sucked in a breath and let it leak out between her lips. A cloud of flies swarmed around her, and she could almost taste the horrible smell rising from the city. She *did* want to go home, so badly it hurt. But she'd only just arrived and hadn't done a thing.

"How long is a decent amount of time to give this before I ask to leave?"

"You *do* want to come home?"

"Of course. It's horrible here." But even saying that made her feel guilty for all the poor people who lived here and the other medics who'd worked here for months.

"Okay," Duncan said. "I'm going to call my father's friend, Major General Knight, at the Ministry of Defense, and arrange for you to be reposted back to the army institute in four weeks."

Relief swept through her, so potent it almost hurt. For the next four weeks she would work all the hours she could and try to take the strain off the other doctors. "That will be great."

"See you in the middle of February, then. I love you, darling. Don't take any risks, and stay safe."

"I'll try. Love you too."

Naomi ended the call and touched the chip of Kindrogan Heart Stone in her pocket. Maybe it was magic, or maybe it was Duncan's love that was the real magic.

As the train to Scotland rattled along, Naomi struggled to keep her bleary eyes open so she didn't miss her stop and end up in Aberdeen.

The last four weeks had been exhausting beyond anything she had ever imagined. The day the rain stopped the rebel forces attacked again with a vengeance, bombing a number of buildings in Rejerrah, and shelling the airfield that night.

They were already busy in the OR when a group of local villagers who'd been caught in a mudslide were brought in. On top of that a NATO patrol ran over an IED and three soldiers were seriously injured. They were stabilized in the field hospital, before Cameron's plane flew them back to the UK for expert treatment at the hospital at Brize Norton.

Naomi had seen more serious trauma in four weeks than most anesthetists encountered in a lifetime. Some doctors seemed to thrive on the demanding work in the field hospital, but Naomi wasn't one of them. The physical and emotional stress and lack of sleep drained her and left her muzzy-headed and faint.

Her phone dinged with a text from Duncan. "How far away are you?"

She texted back: "A few minutes." Then she rose, her body aching with weariness. After the flight back to the UK, she'd climbed straight on a train for Scotland. Her hair was limp and dull, she'd lost weight, and she was none too clean, but she didn't want to be parted from

Duncan a minute longer than necessary.

She grabbed her bag off the overhead rack, and headed along the aisle, holding the seatbacks as the train swayed. The brakes engaged with a tooth-gritting, squeal and she ducked her head to see out the window. Her heart soared as the station sign came into view: KINDER VALE.

The moment the train stopped she pushed open the door and stepped out, her gaze flicking up and down the platform. Duncan leaned against the wall of the ticket office, his faded jeans hugging his narrow hips, his check shirt and vest emphasizing the width of his shoulders. He grinned, and ambled towards her with his arms open.

Tears filled Naomi's eyes as she ran towards him. She dropped her bag and jumped into his embrace, pressing her face against his neck, loving the feel of his strong arms around her. For long minutes they just stood there, holding each other. How she had missed this sense of belonging. She didn't want to travel unless it was with Duncan. Who cared about independence? She wanted love.

"I've been so worried about you, darling." He cupped her cheek in his hand and kissed her. "You look exhausted."

"I am exhausted. That was the worst six weeks of my life."

Duncan picked up her bag, put his arm around her, and led her out to the Kindrogan Estates Land Rover. He opened the door and she climbed in, relaxed for the first time since she had left here after Christmas.

Duncan turned up the heater and her eyelids drooped as they bumped along the rough lane through the pine forest, crested the ridge, and headed along the road beside Loch Kinder. The setting sun gleamed off the distant castle windows, turning them to spots of gold in the granite walls. The snow had melted and

Kindrogan was framed with the green pine forests on the lower slopes of the surrounding mountains. It was a wonderful sight, heaven after the devastation of Rejerrah.

They pulled up outside the back door of the castle and Duncan led her inside. She paused on the threshold to draw in a deep breath of the fresh, cool, Scottish air, mixed with a unique tang that was somehow Kindrogan. This was the smell of home; the smell that clung to Duncan.

"Are you hungry, love? Mrs. Stewart left a venison stew for us."

"I just want to shower and sleep. I'll eat tomorrow."

His gaze skimmed over her. He must have noticed how skinny she was but he didn't say anything."Okay. Come on."

There were clean, dry towels in the bathroom—blissfully without the spots of mold or coating of gritty dust she'd grown used to. She washed the sweat and dirt off her skin, and out of her hair, then wrapped herself in a fluffy bathrobe before crossing the corridor to her bedroom.

Duncan had brought up a tray bearing a bowl of stew and a thick slice of crusty bread. Now she was clean, she did feel hungry. She pulled on her pajamas, climbed into bed with the tray on her lap, and finished the stew in a few minutes.

Duncan returned wearing his pajamas, snuggled in bed beside her, and enclosed her safely in his arms. With his lips pressed against her temple and his warm breath on her hair, she drifted off to sleep—the reassuring beat of his heart beneath her palm.

Naomi woke to light streaming in through the windows onto the bed. She turned over and caught the sweet fragrance of roses. When she cracked open her eyelids, she noticed a vase stuffed with beautiful red blooms on the bedside table. Propped against it was a large gold envelope decorated with red hearts.

"Duncan?" She sat up and glanced around. An assortment of vases filled with red roses filled every surface in the room.

He pushed open the door and came in with a mug in his hand that he set on the bedside table beside the vase. "Good morning, sleepy head. It's nearly noon. I've been waiting for you to wake up and open your card."

At her confused expression he laughed.

"It's Valentine's Day."

"Oh, of course. February 14th." Six weeks after she had left for Africa. "What a lovely surprise."

She relaxed back against the pillows and pulled the romantic card covered in hearts and cute, fluffy bears out of the envelope. "Oh, Duncan, this is so sweet and the roses are lovely. Thank you. I'm sorry I didn't get you anything."

"My darling, all I want for Valentine's Day is you." He sat on the edge of the bed and wrapped his arms around her, kissing the tip of her nose. "I have something else for you."

He slid down onto one knee, pulled a small red velvet box out of the pocket of his dressing gown, and lifted the lid.

A huge emerald surrounded by diamonds winked up at her in the sunlight.

"Naomi Gray, will you do me the honor of becoming my wife?"

Naomi pressed a hand to her heart as it nearly beat out of her chest.

"I know this is quick. I want you to be sure that when I say I love you, I really mean it, forever."

"Oh, Duncan." Tears filled her eyes. "Yes, please."

He slipped the ring on the third finger of her left hand. She threw her arms around his neck, holding her hand up behind his head so she could see the ring. "It's lovely, Duncan. Thank you so much."

"I thought an emerald would match your eyes."

"And the beautiful shades of green in the Scottish countryside," she added.

"I have another surprise for you as well." He drew a couple of sheets of paper from his pocket, unfolded them, and handed them over.

"What's this?" She scanned the pages. Excitement streaked through her. "An adoption application for Holly."

"We don't have to be married to adopt her. I've already started the process."

A little cry of pleasure burst from her lips as emotion welled inside her. Traveling wasn't her dream. This was her dream, to live with Duncan and Holly at Kindrogan. To be this wonderful man's wife, and Holly's mum. Duncan knew her better than she knew herself.

There were no adequate words to thank him so she leaned into his chest, and hugged him as if her life depended on it.

"Are you happy, love?"

"Happier than I've ever been before. I can't wait to have Holly here with us."

"Will you move in with me right away?"

She smiled and stroked a hand over his stubbly cheek. "I'm here to stay. Knowing I was coming back to you and Kindrogan was all that kept me going these last few weeks."

All her life she'd been adrift with no place to call home and no family who cared about her. She'd dealt with that by planning to travel. If she was always moving on, it was easier to forget that she didn't have a home to go to. But Duncan had given her what she'd been missing, a safe harbor, a place to return to where she was loved and wanted.

"I've something to show you, too. Pass me my jacket, will you."

He grabbed it off the chair and handed it over.

Naomi dug in the front pocket, pulled out the chip of Heart Stone, and held it up. "I took a little piece of Kindrogan with me to Africa so I wouldn't forget this wonderful place and Scotland."

"And it brought you back to me."

"It wasn't the Heart Stone that did that, Duncan, it was you. *You* are my heart stone. Wherever you are, my darling, is where I want to be. For the rest of my life."

Epilogue

On a warm August day at Kindrogan Castle, the Mackenzie family and their friends gathered for Duncan and Naomi's wedding. The stone arch on the edge of Loch Kinder was covered in red roses, the sun glinted off the gently rippling water, and Torrie and Bruce dashed around shooing the ducks out of the reeds.

Duncan stood on the lawn by the arch with Holly wriggling in his arms, desperate to get down and join the other children on the ground. She patted her tiny hand against his cheek, her blue eyes pleading for freedom. "Da da da da," she chanted in her adorable little voice.

Holly had started to crawl in June. Now she could move like greased lightning. If he put her down, before he knew it she'd be dabbling in the water at the edge of the loch, or eating something horrible she found on the grass.

Duncan had been given one job, to stop Holly ruining her pretty blue dress. He was determined to keep his daughter clean—or fairly clean. She already had grass stains on the underskirt where he'd put her down for a moment to shake hands with his friends the Knights. He wasn't making that mistake again.

Radley and Cameron Knight and their wives

finished doing their round of hellos and returned to chat to Duncan while he waited for Naomi to appear.

"Holly is such a sweetie; you'd think butter wouldn't melt in her mouth." Radley's wife, Olivia, tickled the tiny girl, making her giggle.

Radley and Cameron looked on with the superior demeanor of fathers who have successfully trained their offspring not to eat worms or roll in mud in their best clothes.

Their father and mother, Major General Knight and his wife, came over and shook Duncan's hand. "Congratulations, I'm glad your fiancé arrived back from Africa in one piece. We're thinking of scaling down the medical facility there or possibly withdrawing altogether. It's become too dangerous."

"Thank you for your help with having Naomi reposted, Uncle George. I was relieved to have her home."

After patting Duncan on the back, Major General Knight took his wife's hand, and they returned to talk to Duncan's father, and the vicar.

"So, are you nervous?" Cameron asked.

"No." Duncan realized that surprisingly he wasn't. He was excited by the future, but not nervous. He'd waited a long time for this day, the day he married the woman he loved. Today the world was set right on its axis, the weather perfect, and Kindrogan at peace.

It was strange to think of a place having emotions, but when he brought Naomi and Holly into the castle it was as if the atmosphere here lightened. It was as if Kindrogan had been waiting for the next generation of owners to arrive, and could now go back to snoozing away the decades.

Duncan checked his watch. Five minutes until the wedding ceremony was due to start. His gaze flicked to the castle entrance, searching for Blair, his best man. He sighed with relief to see his brother striding over, adjusting the Scottish thistle in his buttonhole.

"You made it."

"By the skin of my teeth. Sorry. Flight was delayed out of Rejerrah because of the most recent attack, and I missed my train."

His brother had lost weight and had a few extra lines on his face. It was time he was reposted somewhere less demanding.

Duncan's phone chimed. He pulled it out of his sporran, and checked the screen. Naomi had said she would text him just before she came down.

"I love you and I can't wait to be your wife. XXX Naomi."

Duncan's gaze rose to her bedroom window, a smile on his lips. Naomi waved through the glass. "Hey, munchkin," he said to Holly and raised a hand to point at the window. "Do you see Mummy waving?"

Holly jigged up and down in his arms with excitement, her little hand fluttering in the air. "Ma, ma, ma," she chattered.

"Ladies and gentlemen, the bride is on her way down," Hew announced.

As the bagpipes struck up, the groomsmen, Hew and Lyall, directed people to their seats on either side of the aisle that led to the arch.

Duncan's sister hurried down the aisle in her blue dress, a few shades darker than Holly's. Megan smiled at him and squeezed his hand. "I'm so happy for you, Duncan. We all love Naomi. You chose well. Now it's time to part with your little darling for a while."

Duncan kissed Holly's hair and handed her over.

"Come on my little angel, time to watch Mummy and Daddy get married." Megan carried Holly away.

A few minutes later, Naomi stepped out of the front door of Kindrogan, her slender form encased in sleek white fabric, the bodice covered in sparkly beads. She looked fantastic. Her bouquet of red roses contained tiny blue and white flowers, and green leafy bits that matched the colors in the Mackenzie plaid ribbon around the stems.

His brother-in-law, Daniel Fabian, escorted her slowly down the aisle as the music played. She had contacted her father and asked him to the wedding, but the man hadn't even bothered to reply, so Megan's husband had offered to give her away.

Megan followed a few steps behind the bride, with Holly in her arms holding a little basket of carefully de-thorned red roses. Duncan's mother came next, warming his heart to see her back at Kindrogan, if only for a few days. His niece, Heather, held her hand, toddling along with her flower basket. Duncan's nephew, Fergus, brought up the rear. Like all of the Mackenzie men, he was dressed in a navy jacket with gold buttons, and the Mackenzie plaid kilt.

Duncan's chest tightened with pride. His family made a wonderful sight in their traditional colors—the men in their kilts, the women with the Mackenzie coat of arms on a plaid rosette pinned to their dresses. The sound of the bagpipes filled the air, and Kindrogan Castle stood watch over the ceremony like a benevolent grandfather.

Folds of transparent white net trailed down Naomi's back and wavy wisps of hair framed her face. She smiled at him as she approached, her green eyes shining with happiness.

Daniel kissed Naomi on the cheek and passed her hand to Duncan. The people faded away as he stared into Naomi's eyes. He recited the lines of the marriage ceremony with feeling, putting his heart and soul into his tone as he said the words, "I do."

A gentle breeze blew in off the loch, teasing the golden strands of Naomi's hair as Duncan gazed into her eyes. In a soft, melodic voice, she pledged to love him for the rest of her life.

He slipped the white gold band on her finger beside her engagement ring and she did the same for him.

As the vicar declared them husband and wife, he raised her hand to his mouth and kissed her fingers beside the ring, part of him still not believing that his dream had come true. This beautiful woman really loved him and wanted to spend the rest of her life with him.

"Duncan, my love, my husband." Her fingertips brushed lightly across his cheek. "With you, I've finally found my place in this world."

He put his arms around her and pressed his lips to hers. The fragrance of roses mingled with the scent of Scotland.

"I love you," he whispered in her ear.

"I love you, too," she replied.

"Da, da, da. Ma, ma, ma," Holly shouted.

"I think your daughter approves," Blair said.

"We all approve," Megan chimed in, and everyone cheered as they rose to congratulate the happy couple.

Duncan had thought his wedding day would be the happiest day of his life, but as he watched his wife and daughter laughing and enjoying themselves, he knew this was only the start. Every day would be the happiest day, with Naomi and Holly in his life.

The Army Doctor's Baby

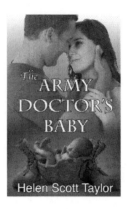

After his wife betrayed him, Major Radley Knight dedicated himself to becoming the best Army doctor he could be, dedicated himself to saving soldiers' lives. When he returns on leave from Afghanistan he is ready for a break. Instead he finds himself helping a young mother and her newborn baby. He falls in love with Olivia and her sweet baby boy and longs to spend the rest of his life caring for them. But Olivia and her baby belong to Radley's brother.

Praise for The Army Doctor's Baby

"This is a sweet romance with a wonderful happily ever after. Highly recommend this read!" Luvbooks

"I loved this sweet, tender romance about a woman in need of a father for her baby and the man who falls in love with her..." Ruth Glick

"Loved the twists at the end of the book. Just the right amount of tension to keep me turning those pages! Totally recommend." Mary Leo

The Army Doctor's Wedding

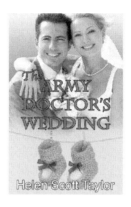

Major Cameron Knight thrives on the danger of front-line battlefield medicine. Throwing himself into saving the lives of injured servicemen keeps the demons from his past away. When he rescues charity worker, Alice Conway, and a tiny newborn baby, he longs for a second chance to do the right thing, even if it means marrying a woman he barely knows so they can take the orphan baby to England for surgery. The brave, beautiful young woman and the orphan baby steal his heart. He wants to make the marriage real, but being married to an army officer who's stationed overseas might do her more harm than good.

Praise for The Army Doctor's Wedding

"Grab a Kleenex because you are going to need it! This is one no romance lover should miss!" Teresa Hughes

"The book starts out with lots of action and holds the reader's interest through to the end. It's a great read!" Sue E. Pennington

The Army Doctor's Christmas Baby

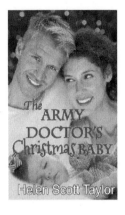

After he loses his wife, army surgeon Colonel Sean Fabian protects his damaged heart by cutting women out of his life. He dedicates himself to his career and being a great dad to his twin babies. When he asks army nurse Kelly Grace to play nanny to his children over Christmas, he realizes how much he misses having a beautiful woman in his life and in his arms. Caring for Sean's adorable twin babies is Kelly's dream come true. She falls in love with the sweet little girls and their daddy, but she's hiding a devastating event from the past. If she can't trust Sean with her secret, how can she ever expect him to trust her with his bruised heart?

Praise for The Army Doctor's Christmas Baby

"...if you want to experience the true essence of Christmas, with the love and understanding that only being with family over the holidays can satisfy, you'll definitely want to experience, The Army Doctor's Christmas Baby." F Barnett

The Army Doctor's New Year's Baby

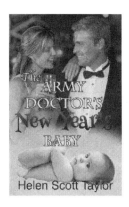

Dr. Daniel Fabian's jet-setting lifestyle as a cosmetic surgeon to the rich and famous left him empty inside. In his quest for fulfillment he followed his brother into the army, to use his medical skills to help soldiers injured in combat. He dedicated himself to his work and cut women out of his life for twelve months. But his commanding officer's beautiful sister Megan Mackenzie is too much of a distraction for him to ignore. Amid the dangerous beauty of the Scottish Highlands, Megan rescues Daniel and shows him he's been searching in the wrong place for fulfillment. His destiny lies in her arms.

Praise for The Army Doctor's New Year's Baby

"The story is a sweet romance with a good dose of sensual tension which I enjoyed tremendously." Reader Forever

"This is a book I'd recommend to all romance lovers!" L Bird

About the Author

Helen Scott Taylor won the American Title IV contest in 2008. Her winning book, The Magic Knot, was published in 2009 to critical acclaim, received a starred review from *Booklist*, and was a *Booklist* top ten romance for 2009. Since then, she has published other novels, novellas, and short stories in both the UK and USA.

Helen lives in South West England near Plymouth in Devon between the windswept expanse of Dartmoor and the rocky Atlantic coast. As well as her wonderful long-suffering husband, she shares her home with a Westie a Shih Tzu and an aristocratic chocolate-shaded-silver-burmilla cat who rules the household with a velvet paw. She believes that deep within everyone, there's a little magic.

Find Helen at:
http://www.HelenScottTaylor.com
http://twitter.com/helenscotttaylo
http://facebook.com/helenscotttaylor
www.facebook.com/HelenScottTaylorAuthor

Book List

Paranormal/Fantasy Romance

The Magic Knot
The Phoenix Charm
The Ruby Kiss
The Feast of Beauty
Warriors of Ra
A Clockwork Fairytale
Ice Gods
Cursed Kiss

Contemporary Romance

The Army Doctor's Baby
The Army Doctor's Wedding
The Army Doctor's Christmas Baby
The Army Doctor's Valentine's Baby
The Army Doctor's Honeymoon Baby
Unbreak My Heart
Oceans Between Us
Finally Home
A Family for Christmas
A Christmas Family Wish
A Family Forever
Moments of Gold
Flowers on the water

Young Adult

Wildwood

Printed in Great Britain
by Amazon